CASSIDY CANE AND THE QUEST
FOR THE DIGITAL HEART

Published in Canada by Engen Books, St. John's, NL.

ISBN-13: 978-1-989473-96-2

Distributed by:
Engen Books
www.engenbooks.com
submissions@engenbooks.com

First mass market paperback printing: December 2020

Cover Design: Ellen Curtis

Slipstreamers Committee:
Amanda Labonté
Ali House
AJ Ryan
Ellen Curtis
Erin Vance
Lauralana Dunne
Matthew LeDrew

CASSIDY CANE AND THE QUEST
FOR THE DIGITAL HEART

JON DOBBIN & JD RYOT

ENGEN
BOOKS

CHAPTER ONE

Shouts echoed through the cavern as Cassidy Cane ran for her life.

It wasn't the first cave she'd navigated blindly – far from it. A knife-edge of a smile danced about her face, her sharp mind recalling her recent escapades thanks to Dr. Gamgee.

"Intruder, halt!" The rough voices slid behind her as she skidded around a corner, a plume of dust rising from her feet.

***

"I know little of this reality," the doctor had said to her as they navigated the crowded station just under Times Square. "I fear that it may be too much like your previous life."

"How do you mean?" Cassidy sidestepped a burly construction worker who had his nose in his phone and rejoined Gamgee. It wasn't like him to attempt to reduce her desire to slipstream. Cautious, yes, he was always cautious, but never this down-putting. She stifled an aggravated sigh.

"Oh… erm… I suppose a word I'd use to describe it is cavernous." Gamgee navigated around an elderly lady who was busy digging into her purse. "I just fear that it may be too much like your spelunking adventures in search of ancient artifacts and trinkets." He hesitated and cleared his throat.

"What's your point, Herbert?"

"Well… I don't want you to become bored with my… with our work," Dr. Gamgee said and lead them on further into the station.

***

Cassidy pushed herself forward. She'd known as soon as she'd stepped foot through the portal that Dr. Gamgee's worries were unfounded. For one, despite its overt appearances, the cavernous place in which she found herself was not a cave. It wasn't a tomb, the bowels of a pyramid, or a viking burial ground. All of which she'd seen firsthand. The place she ran through now, though not a cave, was still quite familiar to her.

A crash sounded beside her as she ran, the sound of a plate breaking, and she chanced a quick flash of her phone's flashlight. An arrow. A snort of a laugh bubbled up, but she forced it back into submission. They can't actually be using bows, could they? A derisive, "ha" was her mind's answer.

Another crash sounded to her left, closer this time. She pushed on.

***

"What train are we waiting for, Doc?" Cassidy had

said and rocked back and forth on her heels. Gamgee was acting strange. They'd walked through the stations of New York for most of the afternoon, Gamgee bent slightly at the hips, his hands behind his back, as if he were following breadcrumbs.

"Wait, you're *not* following breadcrumbs... are you?"

The doctor straightened, a strained smile on his face. "Will you keep it down?" he mumbled through a barely open mouth, his eyes darting to his right. "I'm waiting for him to go on his break."

Cassidy followed his line of sight and saw a large, bald man wrapped in a snug reflective vest over a blue jacket. The subway worker was looking the opposite direction and yawned.

"Herbert, is... is that a security guard?" Cassidy found herself mumbling through a nearly closed mouth as well.

Gamgee nodded and furrowed his ample eyebrows in a manner which told Cassidy to be quiet.

"Good, he's gone," he said after a short silence. "Come, we must be quick." With that he jumped off the platform and onto the tracks. Cassidy could hear him scurrying along in the darkness. With a shrug of her shoulders, she followed.

***

Subway tile exploded next to her head, her already moving arms shot up around her face to keep the shrapnel and dust out of her eyes. She cursed under her breath and scanned the narrow tunnel ahead of her for the next platform. It was her stop.

Another volley of arrows pitched forward around her.

Their aim was terrible, she thought, but the more they practice the better they'll get. She felt an arrow slip by her ear, the violent breeze tickling her skin as it passed. More curses spilled from her mouth.

***

The doctor had lead them to the abandoned station under 18th street. A crumbling, graffitied husk of what had once been one of the first stations open in New York City and possibly America. A thick layer of brown dirt and dust covered the station, scrubbed clean in some places where graffiti artists plied their trade, and adventurous teens sat on a dare. Even those hallowed tenements of usage had a healthy layer of dust as Cassidy and Gamgee crept through the abandoned station.

"Ahh, yes. Here it is," Gamgee said and pointed to a cement wall that was opposite to the once crowded stairs that led from the street above. "It took me some time to figure it out, really." Gamgee ran a thin hand through his hair. "Perhaps it was just too obvious?"

"So, you want me to run through this wall?" Cassidy smiled at the doctor. "This wall. This wall that is located in a train station. Isn't that a little too Harr…"

"Don't," Gamgee held up his hand, cutting her off. "Don't get distracted by that nonsense. What we are doing here is for science, and for the betterment of mankind."

"Okay, okay. So, tell me what you know," Cassidy said through a sly smile.

"As I said, I don't know much. I did a quick inspection, but all I saw was a cave. I suppose the other reality didn't need to rely on subway trains for transport. Funny though, I did see some graffiti, not unlike what we see around us now. It was jumbled and painted over many, many times, but one phrase did stand out. Repeated over and over again: the Digital Heart."

"Sounds made up," Cassidy said, looking around at the myriad of images and words that surrounded them.

"Yes, well, nevertheless. When you explore, take note of this digital heart. See if you can decipher its meaning."

"Will do," Cassidy said and readied herself.

"I don't believe you'll be there very long, but let's say three days tops, eh?"

"Sure, doc. What happens if I'm not back?"

"You know the protocol. We block the entrance and I notify your family."

"Cheery thought," Cassidy patted her satchel and nodded. "Good luck getting something down here to block up this one," Cassidy said and patted the doctor on his shoulder.

"Leave that to me," the doctor smiled and watched her disappear into the solid concrete wall.

***

"It's got to be here somewhere," Cassidy cursed and plunged forward. Light was a commodity in these tunnels. Where were the emergency lights and the sounds of passengers going about their day? Where was the functional bloody station?

Cassidy's shoulder slammed into a column and spun her around; more arrows sped through the air. She fell to her knees, the debris and rock cutting into her pants and legs.

"Damn it," she said and struggled to her feet.

"There they are," the rough voice rose from the shadows at her heels.

Anger washed over her. She grit her teeth and clenched her fists. She wouldn't be captured again. Not this time. She removed her collapsible shovel from her bag. A quick flick of her wrist and it was fully extended. Not long by shovel standards, but plenty long for a club or an axe.

"Psst," a small voice to her left made her jump. "This way." It was the voice of a child. She'd been around two younger sisters for too long to not recognize the playful lilt in a child's voice.

"Who…"

"Hurry, this way," a small hand gripped her wrist and tugged at her.

Cassidy turned back towards her pursuers. It was dark, but she didn't think they had caught up yet. If she had a chance, it was this. She let out a low sigh and allowed herself to be led away, hopefully to safety.

CHAPTER TWO

The child dragged Cassidy to a grate that had been dislodged from the ground between tracks – sewer access maybe or some sort of electrical maintenance shaft. Cassidy couldn't say for sure. They crawled down amongst the shadows; their feet on the access ladder made a metallic echo in the tunnel below them that Cassidy feared would draw her pursuers. The child didn't share her worry.

He was a small boy. Skinny, maybe ten if Cassidy was being generous. His skin was a honey brown under smears of dirt and dust. He had large, kind eyes that were a dazzling golden hazel. He put a finger to his full lips and guided her away from the ladder and deeper into the tunnel.

Time stretched on as they watched the entrance to this access tunnel. Cassidy's adrenaline still thundered through her veins, her fists clenched and ready for a fight. Any minute now the dark shadows holding crossbows would descend and she'd have to fight her way free. But that didn't happen. Instead the whispered voices of those that pursued her passed on, without hesitation.

Cassidy could feel her body relax. It was an aching, restless feeling as the adrenaline subsided. It left her limbs weak, her muscles like jelly and all she wanted to do was sit and eat, or do it all over again.

The boy grasped her hand and she flinched away from him. Her heart raced once more, her hands curled into tight fists, but it faded as quick as it had come on when she stared into the boy's gentle eyes. Cassidy forced a smile and held out her hand, and the boy led her further into the tunnel.

It was dark and Cassidy was having a hard time getting her bearings as she allowed herself to be pulled through the strange underpass. And yet, she had the feeling that they were going in a completely different direction from whence she had initially started her escape. Not that it mattered much to her, she was thankful for finding an escape at all before an arrow had made a pin cushion out of her.

"Hey, kid," she said once she was sure they were a sufficient distance away from the open grate. "What's your name?" Cassidy bent forward, hoping to catch a whisper from the young boy, but her only answer was another tug on her arm to signal her to go faster.

"Come on, kid," she said and gave him some resistance; not enough to stop them completely, but enough to make her point known. "I just want to give you a proper thanks, kid."

The boy shot her an annoyed look and pulled her forward with renewed gusto. Cassidy rolled her eyes in return and kept moving, though she dragged her feet some to let the kid know she wasn't too much of a pushover.

It wasn't long before the kid halted their progress all together. His head swiveled from side to side. The hair on the back of Cassidy's neck stood up, her heart picked up speed again. At this rate, she thought, I might just have a heart attack before even putting up a fight. The thought didn't hit her as funny as she had hoped.

A soft clicking noise came from just beyond a bend in the tunnel. A squeaking noise that was akin to a mouse or rat. Cassidy had had to deal with her share of rodents in her life, and while this new sound was similar, it certainly wasn't any sort of rodent she'd ever heard. *Crap*, she thought, and made to put herself in front of the boy.

As Cassidy moved, the boy made his own set of squeaking noises done with subtle lip movements on the boy's part while he sucked his teeth. *Clever*, she thought.

A solitary figure stepped out of the shadows and beckoned them to continue on. Tall and lean, though broad around the shoulders, the man in the shadows had a crossbow laid across the crook in his arm. He cocked his head upon locking eyes with Cassidy, froze for but a moment, and waved them on. The kid gave her a smile and pulled her forward.

Well, this has been an interesting turn of events, Cassidy thought and reached into her satchel to grasp her shovel – just in case.

***

"My name is Daniel Fletcher," the man who had beckoned them on said with a quick look over his shoulder. Fletcher was an average looking man who had the look of a boy that had to age into a man too quickly. He wore a beard that was in need of a trim, but it was obvious he regularly took care with it and, Cassidy had to admit, it suited him. On top of his head was an ill-fitting stocking cap that he had unnecessarily folded so that it seemed to only perch on his scalp like a strange kippah.

He led them through a large steel door and into a tunnel that was lit by oil lamps and torches. Cassidy had become so accustomed to the darkness of the subway tunnels that she had to keep her eyes lowered to avoid the feeling of being blinded. In the meantime, she had to force her eyes not to squint and they were watering profusely for her troubles. She cursed under her breath, she didn't want her first impression to come across as a weepy damsel in distress. She renewed her grip on her shovel.

"I was surprised that Arturo had brought along a… guest."

"Cassidy Cane," she said, "I'm just glad Arturo here came along when he did." She turned the kid around and squat down to his level. "Thanks Arturo," she said and gave his hand a mighty shake.

"No problem," the boy said, his cheeks darkening some.

"It's a pleasure to meet you, Cassidy, and forgive me for cutting to the point, but what the hell are you doing here?" Fletcher stopped and put himself between Arturo and Cassidy, his crossbow held up and at the ready.

Fletcher's glacial blue eyes were fixed directly on Cassidy, his stare unwavering as he waited for her response. It wasn't an easy question for Cassidy to answer. On one hand, she could go ahead and tell him that she was from another dimension or reality and confuse the man, or she could make up some elaborate lie and hope it made sense for this reality. It wasn't an easy choice. Maybe something more in the middle.

"I'm in search of the Digital Heart, and I only have three days to find it."

CHAPTER THREE

Fletcher and Arturo shared an uneasy glance.

"You're looking for the Digital Heart?" Fletcher's trigger finger twitched on his crossbow.

"Yes, I believe it may be of use in my di– home. My hometown."

"Hometown," Fletcher drew out the word, let it play on his tongue for a moment. "And where might that be?"

"Plainsfield," Cassidy said without hesitation, but upon seeing the beginnings of another question form on Fletcher's lips, added, "Massachusetts. Plainsfield, Massachusetts."

"Massachusetts," Fletcher paused and gave a curt nod to Arturo. The boy backed away into the darkness. Fletcher aimed his crossbow at Cassidy, "Now I know you're lying."

"W-what?" Cassidy took a step back.

"No more of that," Fletcher gestured his weapon at her. "So, what did Beckett intend when he hired you, hmm? I must admit, your performance up to this point was remarkable. That 'I'm-not-a-damsel-in-distress,' but 'I-really-am-a-damsel-in-distress' act really sold the authenticity." A smile curled on one side of his mouth.

Cassidy's fists clenched.

"Then you went ahead and mentioned Massachu-setts," he shook his head, a low chuckle escaped from his chest. "You must be a special kind of stupid."

"First of all," Cassidy said, and tossed her phone at Fletcher's head. He ducked and fired his crossbow, the bolt shooting straight for Cassidy's chest, but Cassidy was already moving. She ran in a diagonal line to cross the short distance to the tunnel's wall. At the last second she jumped feet first toward the wall and kicked off of it to launch herself toward Fletcher. As she did she lashed out with a punch.

Fletcher was about to slip another bolt into his bow when Cassidy's fist landed on his jaw. He sprawled back-wards on the dirt floor, his crossbow landing just out of his reach.

"As I was saying," Cassidy said, her breathing still steady, her heart rate average at best. She frowned. "I'm no one's damsel in distress. Second, what's wrong with Massachusetts?"

Fletcher rubbed his chin. "You can't be serious," he said and let his tongue explore the inside of his cheek.

"Humour me."

"Massachusetts doesn't exist anymore. It's part of the Greater State of Quebec," Fletcher said and rolled his eyes.

"The greater state of…" She'd been to some strange places since she started working with Dr. Gamgee, but the Greater State of Quebec? That was just too much. "But this is New York?"

Fletcher's eyebrows furrowed. "Yes."

"Just New York, or did we become statewide room-mates with some other states?"

Fletcher eased himself up to sitting. "All the way down to North Carolina, including parts of Ohio, Kentucky, and Tennessee."

"Why?" Cassidy said, intending the question more for herself than Fletcher.

"How do you not know this?"

"I'm asking the questions," Cassidy turned her attention back to the man at her feet and sighed. She didn't know much about him, but Fletcher (and young Arturo) were the only people she'd met so far in this new dimension (reality) that hadn't wanted to capture her or shoot her, right away anyhow. Not only that, but they knew this world, and they wanted to help her, until their paranoia got the better of them. If she wanted to find out what the Digital Heart was and get back to her world, she'd need to trust someone. It might as well be this guy.

"How about we start over?" Cassidy said after a moment and crouched down to look Fletcher in the eyes. He gave her a quizzical look and then nodded.

Oh boy, what have I gotten myself into this time? Cassidy thought and helped Fletcher to his feet.

***

They had started walking again, Fletcher leading the way. Cassidy kept the crossbow, just in case. Fletcher had brought them to a halt after about ten minutes of walking and Cassidy heard a continuation of the rodent sounds that she heard earlier. Once they started walking again,

Arturo joined their ranks. He paused once he saw Cassidy with the crossbow, but only shrugged and moved along next to Fletcher.

"So," Cassidy started once they had settled into a good pace. "Tell me all about these new jumbo states."

Arturo shot her a quick glance and then another at Fletcher. The older man just shrugged his shoulders.

"Pretend I've got amnesia," she said to the boy, who gave her a blank look and another shrug.

Fletcher sighed. "It all started on the Night the Lights Went Out. That must've been, oh, thirty years ago, I guess. One minute we were all watching the war unfold on the television; the next it went dark. Everything went dark. It wasn't just the lights either. No, everything electrical seemed to give out. You don't look old enough to remember any of this anyway, but there was a fair bit of panic. I'm sure you can imagine that. One minute there was light, heat, entertainment, power. The next there was none of that. People got scared.

"Well, we all did our own things then. It's amazing to me that we didn't crumble as a people. Instead we pulled it all together. People actually helped one another. Communities came together, towns, cities. Eventually we managed to get word across the entire continent. The lights had gone out everywhere. Still, that didn't stop us. We came together, worked things out and rebuilt. Of course, because there was no electricity, we had to revisit some of our history books for those ideas."

Cassidy hefted the crossbow to have another look at it. She'd studied ancient crossbows in her travels, even one made with cast bronze fittings from seventh century China, and she'd handled her fair share of modern crossbows. With a closer look, Cassidy could tell that the crossbow she now carried was much closer to the ancient design than the modern. For one, the bow string wasn't some synthetic super fibre, but from hand woven hemp.

"We couldn't reach the world outside of America, but we assumed that if it happened here, it happened everywhere, and took some solace that a second attack wouldn't be coming."

"It was an attack then?"

"Oh yes, very much so. I was only a youngster myself back then, but there was a lot of talk around nuclear weapons during the war, but that wasn't what was used in the end. No, in the end it was an..."

"EMP," Cassidy finished his thought for him.

"Yes, that's what it was. Something that took out our technology. I can only assume that it did its job well, probably too well."

Cassidy fingered the phone in her pocket and thought of all of her devices waiting in her satchel. Hadn't she used her phone's flashlight? *I wonder what these guys will say if I start playing some Eminem,* she thought and removed her hand from her pocket. Probably not a good idea to find out.

"So, who is this Beckett you mentioned earlier? The guy you thought I was working for?"

"Well, these 'super states' as you put it—"

"Jumbo states."

"Huh...er...yes. These 'jumbo states' as you put it were created in a way to keep a form of government. It would have been too hard to communicate with all the states and provinces without the use of technology, or I suppose that's what we thought around thirty years ago. So, instead of a Governor or Premier (as I think they were called in Canada) taking one small area, we gave them control over a larger chunk of real estate and they parsed out responsibility to others, usually landowners or the rich. They're usually the same thing."

"So, Beckett is some sort of Feudal Governor?"

"If you say so. He'd rather be called Lord than Governor though," Fletcher said.

"And why would Beckett hire someone like me to interfere with you? Are you a criminal of some sort?"

Fletcher stopped and turned. His face flushed red and his nostrils flared. "Beckett is an oaf and a bully. He has perverted his position in the government," Fletcher said slowly, picking his words carefully.

"And you're what? A rebel, a revolutionary?"

"I'm just someone who believes in what we have built out of this hardship. I can't continue to watch someone pervert all the hard work we've put in to making this state, this continent, seem good again."

A little of both then, Cassidy thought.

"You, or someone like you, would probably be used as a spy. Someone who could infiltrate the inner circle and shut it down or, at the very least, disrupt it and delay operations."

Cassidy let the silence stand for a few minutes. This was certainly the first dimension of its kind. A world that was almost exactly the same as hers, and yet very different. She started to wonder if the people of this world were still able to go out to dinner; would they go dancing?

She also thought about what it would be like for her to be stuck in this reality. Could she survive without Twitter and her podcasts? No automatically heated water in the shower, no pizza delivery during her late nights correcting. No driving, at all. Would she have to get a horse? She thought with no ounce of irony or foolishness.

"Do you mind if I ask you some questions now, Ms. Cane?" Fletcher had cast a quick glance over his shoulder. Cassidy shrugged.

"What do you want with the Digital Heart?"

"That, my friend, is not an easy question to answer. However, to make it a little more easy to understand, I intend to study it. I hope to review the Digital Heart and learn if it can help people from the knowledge I'm able to glean from it."

"You don't even know what the Digital Heart is, do you?" She could see the lopsided smirk he had given her earlier.

"No. No, I don't. Maybe you could fill me in?"

"Well, not much is known about the Digital Heart. Some believe that it is the key to unlocking all the secrets kept by this newly founded government, as unlikely as that is. Others say it is just a computer file that may be a key to restoring the electricity. To be honest, I think they are a load of hogwash."

"I tend to agree. You can't very well run a computer program without any power."

Fletcher shrugged. "Beckett can."

"But didn't you already say that all the power is gone? That we were effectively plunged into a new dark age?"

"I did and we most certainly are, but that doesn't

change what Beckett can do."

"I'm sorry. I don't understand," Cassidy said and shrugged.

"Listen, I may be willing to believe that you aren't an agent of Beckett, but there's only so much I can do to suspend my disbelief. You must know about the chosen ones."

"Amnesia," Cassidy said and pointed to her head. She crossed her eyes at Arturo eliciting a blush and a smile from the boy. "Continue," Cassidy waved her hand at Fletcher.

"Fine," Fletcher said with a deep sigh. "It was about a decade after the lights went out that stories started to circulate. Rumours that the machines were coming back to life, but that rumour soon changed. It was people. Some special people were able to use machines again. Nothing big at first, a pocket calculator, a watch. That was easy to explain away though, because the batteries were not affected by the EMP. Then a blender started running in someone's hands. Next there was a car roaring down the road."

"And Beckett can do that sort of thing?"

"That and more. People like Beckett, able to raise technology from the dead, were able to place themselves in some strategic positions in the new society. Beckett, for instance, as you know, is Lord of the Greater New York State. Though we wish he wasn't. Many believe he became obsessed with power. His power to use technology, and his power over people. He flaunts it, uses it for control. Absolute control." Fletcher led them on.

"Absolute power corrupts absolutely," Cassidy said quietly to herself.

CHAPTER FOUR

The tunnel narrowed as they walked and they were forced to walk single file. Conversation had halted, and Cassidy was fine with that – she had a lot to process. At the end of the tunnel was an iron ladder bolted into the concrete. Graffiti cluttered the walls around it, aged and ugly, the art was chipped in places that obscured its meaning. Nothing denoted the presence of the Digital Heart.

The climb up the ladder was arduous. Cassidy's legs burned from the chase, and her adrenaline had started to dump. She could feel her limbs shake as her energy began to wane. Cassidy silently cursed Dr. Gamgee and his promise of an uneventful journey. He'd bestowed in her a false sense of security. Worse, a false sense of banality. It's not that she wanted the trip to be boring, far from it, it's that she hadn't properly prepared herself.

Cassidy sighed. Excuses, excuses.

***

They emerged onto a basketball court – or what remained of one. Grass crept up through cracks in the concrete, fighting with the broken glass and debris for existence. A rusted out truck was parked over a collapsed chain link fence to one side, and one basketball net was strewn across the centre of the court.

New York City sprawled around her, buildings reached like fingers toward the sky, pointing to something that could not or would not be seen. Though she had never been to this park before, the sight hit home and Cassidy felt more comfortable. New York City was one of a kind. And yet it was different. Her initial elation at being able to recognize something, or being within her own element again, shrivelled and cowered once she was able to firmly plant herself in her current reality. It was the noise – or the lack thereof. No sounds of cars idling, horns honking, or people chatting as they walked. No music blared from an apartment window, no fire sirens screamed by, there wasn't even the sound of footsteps. New York was many things, but quiet was not amongst them. This New York was a ghost. Cassidy shivered.

"Come on," Fletcher said and motioned they go west.

"Where are we going?" Cassidy said once she had caught up.

"Home," Arturo said, and his young voice cracked some. Cassidy gave him a smile.

"In a manner of speaking," Fletcher cut in. "It's more a base of operations, where some like-minded people are able to meet and discuss things candidly. Where we can prepare."

"Sharpen your knives?" Cassidy said, but was only met with a grunt of a response. "So, are all these buildings empty, does anyone live here anymore?"

"Beckett and his cronies live around here," Fletcher waved his hand vaguely. "Not in this area though, if you're worried."

Cassidy shrugged. "Where is everyone else?"

"Most people were moved closer to fields. Easier to provide for yourselves that way. Food is like currency. If you have nothing else to offer, you can at least offer that."

'Don't you find it strange,' was Cassidy's next question, but it died on her tongue. Fletcher had grown accustomed to the dead city and Arturo hadn't known it to be any different. Cassidy had just this morning been travelling the streets and subway tunnels of New York. The real New York. New York as it should be, not some hollowed chrysalis that paraded itself around as New York.

Then again, she had to wonder, was this really her New York? It was a different reality; could that mean that certain things were already different in this city, even before the EMP hit? Cassidy made a mental note; if she had time she'd investigate further. For now, she needed to focus on the Digital Heart.

"So, the Digital Heart is something that Beckett would have in his possession?" Cassidy said.

"I assume so. If the stories are true, then all Governors should have some version of it." Fletcher's head moved from side to side, scanning.

"And where could I find Mr. Beckett?" Cassidy tried to keep up with Fletcher's sight lines, to try and get a glimpse of what he might be looking out for, but he moved too quickly. Too randomly.

"Listen, Ms. Cane, I would love to continue to tell you the very well-known recent history of New York State, but

I've had a long day. I've been punched in the face, and, frankly, I don't feel like talking much anymore. Perhaps you could save your questions until we reach our destination?"

Cassidy shrugged and muttered something about amnesia.

***

The city was as empty as Cassidy had feared. The silence pushed in on her, echoed within her mind. Loneliness also seemed to creep in, a feeling that accompanied the thought of being deserted. Cassidy had been on some digs in the past, some self-appointed missions where she would have begged for time to herself. A moment to allow her to cultivate even a slim thread of clarity. After being present in this spectre of New York, she doubted she would feel that way again.

Life had been drained from this city. Without people living within it, it just became an exercise in monotony. Buildings began to bleed together until New York became a series of stone walls that guarded a maze of streets and alleyways.

Even the vegetation had refused to live there. Cassidy always assumed that in the result of some sort of catastrophic event, that even if humanity were completely wiped out, Mother Nature would make her presence known, that the earth would reclaim what had once been its own. That didn't happen in this New York. Sure, grass grew where the concrete had split. Roots of trees had gone unchecked over the last decade or more and began to jostle some walkways and fences, but nothing like she had imagined. Where were the vines snaking into every crevice, choking buildings with their presence? Where were the wild animals at ease in the formerly oppressive human city? Not here, Cassidy thought.

The base of operations Fletcher had spoken of turned out to be a hollowed out school gym that sat in the middle of a large, chain link enclosed parking lot. The exterior of the building was a mixture of brick and concrete with windows that lined the flat top ceiling and decidedly fewer that were spread out on the lower level. These latter windows were boarded up. That notwithstanding, the building appeared to be in good shape, with obvious repair work done to the roof.

"Arturo, let everyone know that we have a visitor with us, will you?" Fletcher said and patted the boy on the back as he guided him through one of the large metal doors that guarded the entrance to the building. "I'd like to have a word or two with Ms. Cane, please."

They both watched Arturo scramble inside, an obvious excitement growing on his face and manifested in his jittery, hopping steps within the old gymnasium.

"He seems like a good kid," Cassidy said and she smiled after Arturo, but her sentiment was cut short.

Fletcher grabbed her. One of his deceptively strong, thin hands latched on to her bicep, the other dug into her shoulder close to her collarbone, and he pushed her up against the outer wall of the gym.

"Let me set something straight," Fletcher's voice came in whispers hissed through clenched teeth. "While I believe you don't work for Beckett, nothing else you have said since we have discovered you has made a lick of sense. You're hiding something, and I don't care what it is as long as it doesn't get in my way. Remember that." He pushed her back against the wall and took two small steps backwards and held out his hand. "Now if you could hand over my crossbow, I think we understand one another."

Cassidy could feel the rage trying to explode through her fists and into Fletcher's face, but forced herself to let it go. This time. She wasn't sure how many of his people were around, and she wasn't sure that taking her frustrations out on one of their number would endear her to them. She'd have to settle this particular score later, once she discovered the location of the Digital Heart. She nodded to Fletcher and followed him into the gymnasium.

The space had been converted from what was once an undoubtedly large open room into a division of cubicles, makeshift rooms created with dividers, and a lot of chairs with colourful, plastic seats. Cassidy even noted that the pool had been taken over as a classroom of sorts. A chalkboard had been bolted to the centre of the rounding lip of the pool and more plastic-backed desks had been placed arbitrarily around it.

The gym was a hive of activity. At least thirty people bounced from one side of the gym to the other, sharing little tidbits of information as they went, passing on what needed to be done or doing it themselves. Cassidy never thought she would feel so happy as she did when she was stuck in a room with dozens of strangers. It wasn't a friendly welcome for Cassidy though. She was sure that Arturo hadn't spoken ill of her, and Fletcher didn't have much chance to do that if he was so inclined. Still, for whatever reason, she was given the harsh, murderous stares of people who were made paranoid by having to survive in a wasteland that had once been a prosperous city.

"Not a very friendly bunch," Cassidy said as Fletcher brought her to a large stage that stood near the rear of the gym. Subdued red curtains, faded by lack of use, clung to the walls on either side. Arturo had retreated here and was laughing and playing with other children who were kicking a ball around the stage.

"They're focused. We are close to reaching our goal." Fletcher tossed his backpack onto the stage, the ghost of a smile crossed his face as he watched the children playing. He turned and furrowed his brows to Cassidy once more. "They don't need any distractions right now."

"Point taken," Cassidy said, perhaps a little too quickly. "So, tell me where to find the Digital Heart and I'll be out of your hair."

Fletcher frowned. "Not so easily done, I'm afraid."

"You don't know where he is, do you?"

"No. He has many different buildings that he resides in, or is rumoured to reside in. We had been hoping that he was in the train station where we… encountered you, but it seems to have been just another distraction."

"And what will you do when you find him?"

"Whatever it takes to remove him from power." Fletcher weaved his way through the gym, checking in on people, updating them on what had happened on his mission. Cassidy noted that he left out the part where she had to punch him.

"So, what is this? Some sort of rebellion?" Cassidy cast a dubious glance at the burly gentlemen who were repairing crossbow bolts.

"That's as good a name as any," Fletcher said and took a moment to hug an elderly woman who was weaving clothes.

"And what do you plan to do to remove Beckett from power? Are you planning on killing him?" Cassidy heard the strain in her own voice. Part of it was in fear of what this mindless killing would do to Arturo and the children like him. Innocence was a thing to be cultivated, not dashed away. The other part was undoubtedly her own reservations. People had died in her life, and Cassidy wouldn't wish that kind of pain on anyone.

Fletcher hesitated. Those gathered in the gym were waiting for his answer. They didn't make it obvious; no one stopped what they were doing or lifted their eyes to the conversation. But there was tension in the air, something that had settled suddenly, a pressure that needed to be released.

"Only if we have to," Fletcher said with measured words. "Only if he gives us no other choice. As much of a dictator as he is, Beckett is useful, even if only for his ability to use technology. It would be a shame to have to kill him outright."

The tension lifted, people went back to their work. Still, Cassidy stared at Fletcher and tried to read his intentions. Dealing with plagiarizing students and lowballing museum curators gave her a fair bit of experience in identifying a liar. Fletcher was hard to read. He was like a politician, always trying to find the most pleasing answer for the masses; the answer that would get him the most votes on election day. His answer was fine, she thought, but could it be trusted? That she couldn't judge.

"I think we may be able to help one another, Mr. Fletcher," Cassidy said after some time studying the apparent leader of the rebellion.

Fletcher snorted, "Oh really?"

Cassidy's smile broadened. "Yes, sir. I think we can."

***

Cassidy didn't think she would be able to fall asleep. The cot they scrounged up for her was nothing more than a green piece of tarp stretched between metal poles, and the pillow she received was just a rolled-up towel. She'd slept in worse places, on worse things, but that wasn't what kept her awake. It was the worry. The fear that the doctor would close the door before she could return. What if she couldn't find this Digital Heart in three days, what if she couldn't find her way back to the portal in time?

Despite the negative thoughts and worries that flowed through her mind, Cassidy fell asleep and was joined by dreams of dancing arrows, flashing digital numbers, and Dr. Gamgee's face just before rocks fell before the portal and she was stuck in the husk of New York City. Forever.

CHAPTER FIVE

Cassidy woke up with the sun casting a warm sliver of light on her forehead. The gym was quiet. Many of the people who she'd seen the previous day had left during the night. Scuttling away to their own homes, Cassidy supposed. Still, she could hear the distant sound of breathing somewhere around her.

She chanced a look at her phone. A picture of a ragged goat appeared, its head turned to the side and its dark tongue hanging from its mouth. Cassidy smiled. Cans, the goat, always made her feel better.

6:40am. 10% battery.

Cassidy powered down the phone. "See ya later, Cans."

"What cans?" Fletcher said, coming around one of the many dividers that was used to break the gym into sections. His hooded eyes fell on her, bloodshot.

Cassidy pushed her phone into her pocket. "Nothing. Just thinking out loud."

Fletcher shrugged and zipped up his coat. His crossbow was hanging across his back and flattening his backpack. A quiver of bolts hung from the belt at his waist, and

Cassidy noticed that he added what looked like a buck knife to his ensemble, strapped to his left boot in a worn leather sheath.

"Time to go," he said and started off towards the door.

Cassidy groaned, slid out of bed and gathered her things. She placed the strap of her satchel across her chest and held it tight with one hand before she walked after Fletcher. Her other hand dug through the contents, pushing aside her shovel, a flare, and a hand brush; she felt the cool, smooth plastic shell of what she needed. With any luck she'd be home later today, tomorrow at the latest. A smile grew on her face.

They set out into the quiet streets of the dead New York, the sun lighting their way. Fletcher was quiet, his broad shoulders straight as he strode forward, his head scanning for any movement. Cassidy tried to follow his lead, but it didn't suit her.

"You really don't want to find this place, do you?" Cassidy said, trying to distract from the lonely sound of their footsteps on the cracked asphalt.

"How do you mean?" Fletcher glanced over his shoulder at her, a sneer on his thin face.

"Just the two of us..." Cassidy gestured around and shrugged.

Fletcher allowed himself a short chuckle. "The others left earlier. We spread out in teams of two, hoping to find some sign of Beckett."

"Where are we heading?" Cassidy said, now walking alongside of him. Fletcher was taller and had longer strides than her, but she was accustomed to having to keep up with taller people. To surpass them. It was a little more effort, but nothing that'd make her wheeze.

"Not too far from the subway station where we found you, actually."

"Thought there was nothing there?"

"Well, maybe not. He'd stationed some guards there, as you know, so perhaps he is nearby. It isn't entirely outside the realm of possibility…"

"But it's slim," Cassidy said, nodding her head.

Fletcher shrugged. "We'll see."

They continued on through the surreal empty streets of New York. Signs that Cassidy didn't recognize still hung from their buildings, rotting. Signs that featured a sale on CDs and cassette tapes, comic books, designer jeans. The designer names didn't sound familiar, but then again, Cassidy hadn't been one for anything too fancy. Too expensive meant more guilt when she got them dirty, and Cassidy always got her clothes dirty. Mud, dirt, blood. Cuts, scrapes, tears. Cassidy's clothes didn't last long, so she bought cheap. It worked for her.

"Not many clunkers around here," Cassidy said to keep away the sound of their feet slapping and its echo. It was true, however. The last broken down car she had seen was the old rust bucket of a truck she saw in the basketball court.

"When the lights went out, we tried to keep the roads clear. At first it was just to push them to the side of the road, enough so that people could drag their belongings behind them without having to contend with the obstacles. I remember my dad had me help move our car. He sat me behind the wheel. Allowed me to steer. That was the closest I ever got to driving."

"What happened to them since then?"

"We try to push them into more open spaces. The parks, the stadiums. We move them there to rot and hope none of the garbagemancers come around and decide to use one."

"Garbagemancers?"

"Heh, yes. It was a name we came up with for those still able to use technology. They bring garbage back from the dead, get it?"

Cassidy gave herself a moment to process the reference. "Oh," she said, excited. "Like a Necromancer. Lord of the Rings?"

Fletcher tapped the side of his nose and chuckled. Cassidy joined him. Soon the decrepit alleys and side streets filled with their laughter, echoing it back at them. It sounded as though there were hundreds of people laughing around those buildings.

A stone fell and it all stopped.

Fletcher had his crossbow in front of him in a split second; Cassidy had her shovel in her grip, following his lead.

"What?" she said, her eyes narrowed, looking around with him. "What was it?"

"I don't know. Not much falls around here anymore," Fletcher said lamely. "It's just a feeling."

Cassidy nodded. She knew about gut feelings. Any archaeologist worth their salt knew about those feelings. Down in the desert, or the jungle, or a mountainside, where the only option is to take that leap of faith and find your quarry, or pack it in and go home, you learned to trust your gut. Cassidy couldn't feel it this time, but that meant little to her. As her father used to say, "not my pig, not my problem". She was in a different reality, a different place. Her gut wasn't as accustomed to it as Fletcher's was.

"It must have been a rat," Fletcher said and stowed his crossbow, his eyes still peering into the darkened windows of the buildings around them. With a sigh, he lead them on.

They moved away from the commercial district and stumbled into the suburbs. It wasn't a particularly posh part of New York, the buildings old and without the charm of the brownstones that Cassidy associated with New York suburbs. Eventually apartment buildings turned into more traditional houses, but the last thirty years had been even harder on them than their stone counterparts. Few remained unscathed, many had fallen in on themselves, and even those left standing sustained holes with both their doors and windows missing.

"Do you really think Beckett would set up shop around here?" Cassidy said, eyeing a trio of houses that had fallen in on each other.

"No, but this way is clear. The train station where we found you is just over there," Fletcher pointed west. "We're heading that way," he pointed towards some tall buildings in the distance.

"We're circling around?"

"More or less. It's my belief that Beckett isn't hiding, as much as he is enjoying opulence. Tall buildings, penthouse suites. He wants to be a king in his castle. His decoys are more so he will be left alone than anything else."

Cassidy nodded. It was a fair assessment. She didn't know this Beckett, but from what Fletcher said, he was likely a narcissist and power hungry. Having his own personal hotel and penthouse suite might be the closest he could get to a castle in New York. If they asked Cassidy, who'd been in dozens of old castles, she'd have told him he was better off in a skyscraper anyway.

***

Fletcher suggested a break on a section of freeway just before re-entering the city proper. The freeway was still littered with vehicles, though most had been burned out or destroyed in some other way. Fletcher guided them to the broadside of an old tractor trailer, the shipping container that it had been carrying hung askew with one edge on the pavement. The rest made an awkward stretch into the sky.

"Not your first time here," Cassidy pointed out the remnants of small fires and garbage that was discarded under the shadow of the container.

Fletcher shrugged, "I'm sure many people have used this place. The trailer provides some shelter from the wind and weather, and if anyone was looking from the city they wouldn't have a clear view."

"And you could have a clear view of whatever was coming the other way," Cassidy muttered and leaned against one of the nearly deflated tires of the truck.

"Just so," Fletcher nodded and squat down in front of the pile of ash that remained from a previous fire. He arranged his things around him and took two clear bottles from his pack and tossed one to Cassidy.

Cassidy drank deeply, and sighed.

"Now that we're alone, do you want to elaborate about where you're from and what you're doing here?" Fletcher said after his own long draw of water.

"Does it matter?" Cassidy tried to avoid Fletcher's gaze and studied the bombed out cars that surrounded them. Fire bombs, maybe even Molotov cocktails.

"Would it matter if you told me?"

Cassidy flashed a smile, but it faded fast. She could still feel the bruises where he'd grabbed her the day before. "I think so," she said after a brief silence.

"Call it a professional curiosity," Fletcher paused and drained his bottle.

"I think, for now, it's enough to say that I'm not from around these parts. You help me get that Digital Heart, and I'll tell you more. Deal?"

"If you help me find Beckett, the Digital Heart is yours. Still, I'm not sure why you're so confident you can find him."

"What can I say," Cassidy shrugged, "I'm feeling lucky."

***

They scoured two hotels and half of a swanky apartment building. Each of the hotels were deserted, picked clean more like. The only things left were those that were nailed down. The apartment building had the opposite problem. It had too many things. Shopping carts (for some reason) were piled in the entrance way, more cluttered the stairs. So much so that it forced them to turn back, much to Fletcher's chagrin.

As they moved on, Cassidy had the sudden realization that this wasn't her New York. She'd never spent much time in her reality's New York; did the tourist thing from time to time and took in the big sights. She didn't think much of the strange layout she'd witnessed up to this point. She'd never been to the outer edges of New York, never cared to see them. But this stretch of the city, the big buildings, the tall skyscrapers, she'd been there, and this wasn't it. The Woolworth Building, the Chrysler Building, they weren't there. She couldn't even see them from the skyline. This wasn't her New York.

"We'll try here," Fletcher said and pointed to a high-rise that reminded Cassidy of a certain president elect in her reality. She shivered and suppressed an involuntary gagging.

As they made their way to the multi-door entrance, Fletcher did a poor job of fighting off his dejection. Despite his faults, Fletcher was dedicated to his cause. And from what Cassidy could tell, it was a good one. Liberty, justice, rights – they were all worth a fight. She focused a lot on her own crap back at home. Focused on her career, on the next artifact, the next adventure, the next thrill. Sure, she signed petitions for her students, she donated when she could, but did she ever have to fight like this? She wasn't so sure. Now, here she was, helping a cause, albeit in an indirect way. It felt good.

No worries, Fletch, Cassidy thought, *I haven't brought out my secret weapon yet.* She patted her satchel.

Fletcher moved in on the doors but stopped himself so suddenly that Cassidy almost came up solid against his back. She wanted to ask him what was up, but he hissed her to silence.

Cassidy stepped back and took a long look at their surroundings. Nothing stood out, but something was off. She could feel it now, her gut signalled something was amiss. The air was thick with an apprehensive silence that promised trouble and violence. Cassidy reached in her bag and pulled out her shovel.

"You feel that?" Fletcher whispered, his crossbow loaded, its sight up to his eye as he panned the deserted streets.

"Yeah, I feel it," Cassidy said. She felt it and she didn't like it.

An arrow arched through the sky, dull sunlight glistening off its metal head. With a curse Cassidy jumped headfirst and rolled to her feet, leaving the arrow to snap on the pavement where she had just been.

"Cover," Fletcher said. "Get to cover!"

Cassidy was already running. Arrows started to fall from the sky, black dots that might have been a hard rain. They crashed with harsh crunches that reminded Cassidy of the ugly hail they sometimes got in Plainsfield. With sudden inspiration, she put her shovel blade over her head, and choked back a laugh. *Some rain cap you have there*, Cass, she thought and dove into the alley beside the hotel.

Fletcher dove in behind her, his bolt still notched in his bow.

"Can you see them?" Cassidy chanced and strained to look over Fletcher's shoulder.

Through a stream of curses Fletcher answered in the

negative.

"Well, I guess we know we're in the right place," Cassidy said and started to look around. Fletcher shrugged and tried to get a better look at their assailants.

Arrows still pelted the street at the entrance of the alley. The alley itself was narrow, but it was empty. Long gone were the dumpsters and garbage cans that may have housed themselves there in the past. All that remained of that long-ago time was a high chain link fence that guarded the rear exit. Not a huge inconvenience, but Cassidy figured that whoever was firing arrows would be working to surround them. The longer they stayed there, the easier it would be to hold them up; to encircle them.

"We have to go," she tugged on Fletcher's sleeve and jerked a thumb towards the fence.

Fletcher shook his head. "I need to know if this is another decoy or if Beckett is here." Fletcher took a blind shot around the corner and nocked another bolt in his crossbow.

Cassidy turned to let loose another stream of curses and stopped herself midway. On the fence, one leg over the top and two hands gripped for purchase on the crossbar was a young man. He'd frozen when she turned his way, just as she'd frozen. He had on a grey cap, almost like an old aviator's hat with ear flaps and goggles. The rest of his outfit matched his hat and was a muted grey right down to his boots. His face was soft and warm with two rosy cheeks and a trimmed beard in the style of those old pictures of Shakespeare. He wore an expression of a child being caught stealing a cookie from the cookie jar. Cassidy had a moment to wonder how Beckett managed to accomplish outfitting his men in a matching wardrobe before their stalemate was broken.

"Jones, get your ass over that fence. Now!" It was a series of harsh whispers. Whispers that Cassidy was sure she wouldn't have heard if she wasn't looking at poor Jones with his mouth squirming into a sheepish grin.

"Sorry Jonesy," Cassidy said and rushed the young man. Shaking his head, Jones put out his hands in surrender. *Too late*, she thought, and slugged him a good one with her shovel, sending him back over the fence.

She barked a laugh like a challenge at anyone else who attempted to crawl over the fence and saw two more men (both in grey) pick up Jones and drag him out of the alley on the opposite side.

Cassidy turned back to Fletcher. She wanted to draw him over, to reiterate their need to escape, but he was distracted firing his crossbow and cursing into his messy beard. Smile faltering some, she realized that the men she'd just driven from the alley were likely waiting in the opposite street for them to emerge in escape, only to capture them or fill them with arrows.

"Damn it," she said and turned in a circle fuelled by frustration. Her satchel swung out from her side and came down hard on her hip.

"Damn it!" she said again, rubbing where the satchel had landed.

Her satchel.

She looked back at Fletcher, his attention still on the arrows that were now only imitating a pitter-patter of rain. She shrugged.

"No time like the present," she said to herself and

pulled out the EMF detector.

The device she held in her hand, the electromagnetic field detector, wasn't high-tech. Just bigger than the size of her palm, encased in a thick black plastic, with four simple buttons and one screen that was now blank, the EMF didn't look impressive. It wasn't even something that she had intended on taking with her. It was a joke gift given to her by one of her students. EMF detectors were supposed to pick up on ghosts. The theory was that if a ghost was trying to manifest in the area it would draw on the electromagnetic energies around it in order to get the power to do that. Like gathering its chi, Cassidy supposed. Of course, it was all bullpatookey. Her students knew she didn't believe in ghosts, or goblins, or curses for that matter. What kind of archaeologist would roam around in old tombs if they believed in that sort of thing? So, it was a joke. Ha-ha, very funny. She'd shoved it in her bag and forgot all about it.

In a world where there was absolutely no electricity, and no possibility of electromagnetic fields, it could sure as hell detect anyone who could control (was controlling) that energy. In a way, this dead world was the perfect testing ground for an EMF detector. At least that was what she was hoping for. She just had to get close enough, and hope that ghosts didn't really exist.

Cassidy switched on the EMF and saw its dull, green display screen come to life. Numbers began to fluctuate, up and down, but she wasn't worried about that. The device needed to get itself accustomed to its environment – she hoped.

Keeping her back to Fletcher she manoeuvred herself

closer to the building they'd meant to explore. 0.0 blinked at her. She held it to the beige PVC-like pipe that stood out on the wall and got the same result. She bent down and held the EMF toward the ground. It was a long shot, she knew, but she wanted to give it try. Nothing, again.

She looked over her shoulder at Fletcher, who returned her stare with a curious look. He seemed about ready to tell her the coast was clear when another arrow crashed against the wall closest to him. A curse filtered through his moustache and he went back to loading his crossbow.

Not here, she wanted to tell him, but how could she begin? *Not here Fletch, I used my doodad to check electric fields and it said nadda. Oh, what's that? Yeah, I have some pieces of tech that still work. No, I'm not a garbagemancer, thanks for asking though.*

Cassidy turned to walk towards him, a sigh cascading out from her chest, when a flicker of movement in her peripheral vision caught her attention. The EMF lit up.

She brought the device up and looked at it. 2.5 flickered there for a split second. 2.6 replaced it briefly and then 2.5 again. She cast her eyes to the building on the other side of the plaza. Another hotel, smaller than those they'd already scoured perhaps, and certainly smaller than the obelisk beside them, but pleasant to look at all the same. There was something going on in there though. Beckett was putting his abilities to good use.

"Hey," Cassidy said after she had stowed her EMF away in her satchel. "I think I found him."

Fletcher's head snapped toward her so quickly that she thought he may have given himself whiplash. He was on his feet just as fast.

"What do you mean?"

Cassidy nodded her head to the other building. "He's in there."

Fletcher's mouth hung open, not unlike a surprised Mr. Jones when he was found trying to ambush them just a few minutes before. "How...how can you be sure?"

Crap, Cassidy thought. She hadn't really decided on a plausible story. Chalk poor planning up to excitement. She looked around, and her story fell into place.

"See there," she said and pointed to an old grey security camera. They had gone out of fashion a long time ago on her world, replaced by much smaller, much rounder cameras. Thankfully this big, square model was still in non-use in this world; and still so apparent.

"I saw it move. Like it was trying to get a bead on us." Sure it was a lie, Cassidy thought, but it was a white lie. It saved her and Fletcher some trouble, and it solved their problems.

"He's using cameras?" Fletcher said, his brow bent in a scowl as he watched the camera. He brought his crossbow to his shoulder, took careful aim, and put a bolt in the eye of the unmoving camera.

"Good job," Cassidy heard herself mutter, but what she really wanted was to bust in and get the Digital Heart and get back to her world. Fletcher was ahead of the game now, there wasn't much more help she could offer.

"We have to get back to base. We have to plan our attack."

Cassidy's stomach sank. Plan an attack?

"Can't we just sneak in and grab the Digital Heart?" she said in a near whisper.

"No, we need a plan. If we are going to overthrow Beckett, we need a plan and we need people."

Cassidy shrugged. It made sense, but she would still rather just grab the Heart now while they were here.

"Come on," Fletcher turned to her, his face a maniacal mask of joy and excitement. "I think I can find us a way. Stay close and run fast." He laughed as he launched himself out of the alleyway. Arrows flew, but they were few and far between. Cassidy followed but looked back at the modest hotel, hoping to see it again soon. She only had two days left.

CHAPTER SIX

They ran out of the alley, the number of arrows now crashing around them amounted to a light drizzle. Cassidy smiled. They didn't need much room, they just had to get amongst the buildings, play a game of hide and seek, and hopefully wait out Jones and his buddies. After all, they seemed easy enough to trick in the subway tunnels.

Despite the dwindled number of arrows flying, Fletcher took to zigzagging through the street to make himself a harder target to get a bead on. Cassidy followed suit. When in Rome, she thought. She hadn't seen Fletcher book it before. Her times with him up to this point were long, disciplined and slow hikes through the decimated urban landscape. Just like everything else about him, his movement had been reserved; calculated. Now, with reason behind him, Fletcher ran like a gazelle. His long legs pumped with precision and training, something that she'd only seen in the star athletes at her university. Those athletes that were bound for the Worlds', maybe even the Olympics.

Fletcher could run, but Cassidy wasn't about to let him show her up.

Where Fletcher bounded over obstacles, Cassidy either pushed through them or slid atop of them, letting her momentum push her along. When Fletcher gave small spaces a wide berth, Cassidy moved through them. They each played to their advantages, and it kept them at a fairly even keel. Until they discovered the real reason the arrows had almost stopped.

Almost three blocks away from where they were attacked, a dozen men dressed in grey from head to toe stepped into their path. They both skidded into a stop, nearly toppling into one another. They all wore the same outfit that Jones had worn when Cassidy had clocked him with her shovel; grey hats, grey double-breasted coats buttoned to the throat, and grey gloves. The only one that stood out amongst them was a hatless man that stood in the centre of all the others. He was bald, his face bare to match his head, but he had a pair of old Ray Ban Aviators resting on the tip of his nose. Blue eyes blazed from behind them in measured aggression.

Most of these men had bows, two had crossbows to match Fletcher, but the man in the centre had a gun. It was a silver Glock, if Cassidy wasn't mistaken. She was thankful that it wasn't an AK-47 or a M-16, but really, a Glock was more than enough.

Guns, Cassidy thought. Why hadn't she seen more guns? More importantly, why hadn't she thought to question it earlier? *You were too busy avoiding arrows*, she consoled herself, but she didn't think that excuse held a lot of water.

"It is the will of his Lordship, Quinne Beckett, of the Greater New York State, that you are to be placed under arrest," the bald man said. The gun was still pointed to the ground, but that didn't give Cassidy any sort of ease. "Toss your weapons to the ground and surrender peacefully. Failure to do so will end in your death."

Baldy's gun wasn't raised, but the bows and crossbows of his companions were as they moved forward. Cassidy tightened her grip on her shovel, but she was brought around by the clatter of Fletcher's crossbow to her left.

"What the hell are you doing?" Cassidy said gaping at Fletcher.

"Not dying." Fletcher stripped his backpack off and threw it next to his discarded crossbow; his bolts came next.

"I thought you said he was a tyrant, a dictator?" Cassidy could feel her face flush. "Where I come from, men like that, they wouldn't hesitate to kill."

"Well, I'll just have to make sure that we are worth more to him alive than dead," Fletcher said with a subtle grin. "Besides, we're supposed to be back at the base tonight. If we don't check in someone will be along." He said this in a whisper, his eyes on the grey coats walking towards them.

"Rescue party?" Cassidy said, thinking of the number of children and senior citizens she'd seen just the day before.

Fletcher shrugged. "More likely to pick up our bodies, but when they get here…"

"You know what, I'll handle this myself." Cassidy took her cellphone out of her pocket and prayed that it hadn't died since this morning.

The phone flicked to life with the white startup screen,

the startup jingle rose above the muted footsteps of the grey jackets. They paused. Each one coming to a stop, their heads raised in confusion as they tried to understand and pinpoint where the music was coming from.

"Behold, peasants," Cassidy said and switched on her phone's flashlight. "I am a garbagemancer, here to raise technology from the dead and rule over you!"

The grey jackets fell back a step, even Baldy, with his Glock and his Ray Bans, stopped in his tracks. Cassidy would have smirked if she couldn't feel the intensity of Fletcher's gaze on the side of her face.

"Another garbagemancer?"

"Does Beckett know about this?"

"Where did she come from?"

The muttering echoed through the streets as each grey coat turned to Baldy for guidance. For his part, Baldy seemed to be maintaining his cool, and that worried Cassidy. He stared straight ahead at her (not her, her flashlight) and pushed his sunglasses up on his nose. At his side, he thumbed back the hammer of the Glock.

Cassidy's upraised hand wavered. *That's not good,* she thought.

"She only has a flashlight," he said with a southern drawl, which was somehow more surprising than anything else she'd encountered over the last couple of days.

"Run," Cassidy said and threw her phone at the grey coats.

It may have only been a flashlight, but it still sent those big burly men on the back peddle. Cassidy bolted into the building closest to her, and dove into the darkness.

She ran down the length of a hallway, not realizing

that Fletcher wasn't with her until she came to an abrupt stop, her face introduced to a wall.

Tasting the blood that ran from her nose, Cassidy groped her way to standing once more, and turned back towards the entrance. Pale light pierced the dirty windows, dust filled rays of light zigzagged the room, but none reached the back of the room where Cassidy stood in gloom and shadow. Fletcher hadn't come with her.

Cassidy's mind raced. Was he shot? No, she didn't hear the gun go off. Pierced by an arrow then? No, the grey coats had been spooked and scattered, they wouldn't have had time to nock an arrow. *Was it me? Maybe,* she thought. *Maybe he thinks I'm exactly what I said out there. A liar, a traitor.* Maybe he thought it would be better dealing with the devil he knew.

The door swung open and the daylight spilled in. The silhouette of a man darkened the opening.

"Fletcher?"

The gunshot was deafening in the enclosed space. Cassidy brought her hands to her ears and ran to her left, hoping another wall wouldn't impede her escape.

Another shot rang out, muted by the effects of its predecessor. Cassidy ducked down and flailed into a hallway with a bank of elevators to the right and a set of stairs to her left. There was a small window at the end of the hallway that allowed scraps of light in, but it seemed so far away, and Baldy was right behind her. Cassidy took the stairs.

Running up the stairs two at a time, Cassidy pulled herself along with one arm, taking the corner of the twisting stairwell with the agility of a lazy cat. She threw herself into the opposite wall, her shoulder impacted and aided in her rebound as she headed up the stairs to the next level.

Light filtered in through the many windows that were broken open, their glass glittered the floor. A fire exit glared at her from the end of a hallway on the opposite side of that level and she ran to it, the thudding footsteps of the gun-toting bald man echoed up the stairs behind her.

Cassidy thundered across the empty floor; each footfall made her wince; she knew she was giving away her position. Her only other option was to duck into one of the empty rooms and hope Baldy wasn't patient nor thorough enough to check every room. Cassidy didn't want to take that chance. Not only wasn't it smart, but it gave the other grey coats time to recover from the slight shock they may have had.

Where the hell was Fletcher?

A grey clad arm shot out of a room to her right, its thick fingers wrapping around her bicep with ease. Cassidy was pulled back in mid-run so viciously that her legs flailed into the air.

"Where are you going, girl?" The grey coat's voice was gruff. It bristled like his beard, under green eyes. In his other hand he held a thick bow made from a bone white wood, shellacked and obviously cared for. He pulled her in close, his breath warm on her face. She could hear the stairwell door swing open somewhere behind her. Baldy had arrived.

"Just trying to get some fresh air," Cassidy said and drove her knee into the large man's groin. The effect was immediate. With nothing more than a whimper and some deep breaths, he fell to his knees and released his grip on her arm to console himself, rolling on the floor in the fetal position.

"Stop!" The southern twang of Baldy rose up behind her, the distinct click-clack of his Glock's slide being made ready for fire.

Cassidy blew through the fire exit, the bang of the handle on the wall drowned out by another gunshot from behind. The bullet impacted in the wall next to her, dust and wood particles spraying her right side.

Her thighs hit the railing of the metal fire escape and she almost fell headfirst into the alley below. The door swung shut behind her, but Baldy was on his way. She could go down, but the rest of the grey coats were down there (perhaps Fletcher too?).

Cassidy took a deep breath and ran up the fire escape, the clanging of the metal steps rang into the air, and she thought she heard the frenzied shouts of the grey coats coming from the front of the building. She couldn't look back to see if they were coming. The fire escape door slammed open behind her.

She made the top of the brick building in a few minutes, the hurried steps of Baldy behind her. Instead of taking to the roof on her feet, Cassidy rolled over the edge and turned herself to face the stairway. Her hand dipped into her satchel and pulled out her shovel once more, another flick of her wrist and it popped open.

Baldy came up the stairs with reckless abandon, his bald head caught the sunlight as it breached the edge of the roof. He came so fast that he didn't notice Cassidy there until he was half way up the stairs, and by then it was too late.

Cassidy lashed out with the blade of her shovel. She had been aiming for his gun, but at the last second he moved his hand, defending his weapon. Instead, the shovel's blade swung wide, the force dragged Cassidy forward, off-balance.

A curse flew from Baldy's mouth, himself off balance, as he brought his gun back around in a panic. The gun fired twice, dust flew just wide of Cassidy and she pushed herself to the side, lashing out with her shovel once more. The shovel glanced off Baldy's gun hand, scraping off the muzzle of the silver Glock. Again he pulled his hand back, but he was steady.

He didn't fire again, instead he made a grab at the shovel. His long, thin fingers reached out, their tips scraping the handle as Cassidy pulled it out of his reach.

Baldy, his eyebrows furrowed behind his aviators, brought his Glock back up. He gripped it in two hands to steady himself and took aim. Cassidy read his movements and brought the shovel up like an uppercut. The shovel hit the butt of the gun and sent it, and Baldy's hands, into the air. Another shot rang out as a bullet cut through the sky. Baldy refused to let go. Cassidy spun herself around and slammed the flat end of her shovel into Baldy's stomach.

He bent forward, his breath pushed out of him in a wheeze. Cassidy could see his grip loosen on the Glock, but he refused to let it go. His Ray Bans, however, had escaped his face in the scuffle, lost somewhere between the roof and the ground below.

With a frustrated grunt, Cassidy pushed the already off kilter grey jacket over, sending him over the small flight of stairs. He landed with a groan at the junction between the stairs up and stairs down, gun still in his hand, but squirming in pain.

"That'll have to be good enough," Cassidy said through gulping breaths.

More shouting came from below, the angry voices of the regrouped grey coats trying to decide what to do next.

They'll be coming up through the building, she thought. They'd come up the dark stairs see the big man on the floor and he'd guide them to the fire escape. They'd find her, and soon.

Cassidy cast a quick glance at the neighbouring buildings. She flirted with the idea of making the jump to one of them, but the space was too much, the alleyway too large.

"I've jumped farther," she muttered as she turned to take in her surroundings.

It was a flat, empty roof, save for one large metal compartment that probably housed air conditioning or venting of some sort. Cassidy checked around the metal box, her hand sliding over the cracked and scaly rust that plagued its corners and edges. A PVC pipe crawled along the ground away from it and disappeared over the edge of the roof.

Cassidy looked over the edge following the PVC pipe to its end. There were some hard angles in the pipe's descent, but it looked to go all the way to the bottom. With a sigh and a shrug, Cassidy started the climb downward, cursing to herself for not packing a length of rope.

Sweat coated her forehead, she could feel it roll down her back and her t-shirt clung to her ribs and stomach when she finally hit the ground. The grey coats were shouting from the rooftop, blame of her disappearance shifted back and forth. With a smile she stole off into the shadowy alleys and side streets. As she made her way into the unfamiliar, abandoned city the raspy voice of Baldy wormed its way through the buildings, followed her and tried to grip her with thin, wormy fingers. It was followed by the loud bang of a gunshot, silencing everything.

CHAPTER SEVEN

Cassidy moved quickly. She dipped behind cover when she could, but there was precious little of that going around. It was obvious that in the years since the EMP blast there had been a massive clean-up. There was really no other choice. It wasn't the end of the world, after all. Life went on, people needed to live and work and build and grow. The apocalypse was never going to be like it was portrayed in movies and books. Humans were survivors, and more than that, they thrived on community, no matter how splintered that instinct had become over the years.

Cassidy had read about different parts of her own world, when things got downright apocalyptic, people joined together and solved the problem. They took care of each other. She bet that was what happened here. Whether it was Fletcher's handful of rebels moving vehicles out of the road, or some other group clearing the dumpsters to melt down or for some other use. The people here made it easier and safer for each other.

So, what happened after that?

Government was reinstated. Granted it was a crude

feudal type government, but it put one person over an-other and that's when everything started to break down. As much as humans were great together in a pinch, when power was evoked and given, when one man or woman was placed on a pedestal above others, it caused tension. Oh, it probably gave some a feeling of comfort. Those peo-ple would accept their place in the world, but there would always be those 'what if' thoughts.

What if I was in charge?

What if I didn't have to pay my taxes?

What if I had more land?

It was the 'what ifs' of the commoner and the glut-tony for power of the powerful that caused tension. That tension caused arguments. It caused fighting. It caused wars.

Then the garbagemancers came along and that added another level of power and 'what if'. Theirs was a natu-ral power that most couldn't overcome or match. Didn't mean that people wouldn't try.

The government leaders were quick with the appear-ance of sharing power. The garbagemancers were made into landholding lords, given freedom to do what they wanted and the authority to back it up. Though Fletcher never told her as much, Cassidy was willing to bet that even with lordly power, they still owed a monthly tithe to the President of America (or whatever he was called in this world).

They tossed power to their subordinates like candy to children, but the candy was from a bargain bin at the dol-lar store. The powerful didn't like it and wouldn't miss it.

Cassidy was willing to bet that Fletcher and his band of revolutionaries were just one of many across the country, maybe the world. They didn't know eachother existed, but they all played by the same rule. A rule based on that instinct they experienced when the world first went to squalor: help each other, build, live. Hope, too. Maybe Fletcher and his group could actually pull it off.

Fletcher. Part of her thought that he may have been the recipient of that one gunshot she heard as she fled, and another thought it was just Baldy airing his tension. Then again, it could have been meant to draw her back to see if Fletcher had been shot. Or maybe….

"Stop it," she said and put her focus back on her escape.

Cassidy moved down another dark alley, her legs and arms screamed in protest, and she forced herself to sit in the shadows where one building joined the next. She regretted it immediately. Her back ached between her shoulder blades, her shoulders quivered, even her buttcheeks screamed in pain.

"I need to get back to the gym," she said and ran a hand through her hair, pushing it back and out of her face. "Maybe a haircut too."

To hell with it, when you get out of here treat yourself to a spa day. Gamgee can pay for the extra long massage.

Gamgee. She needed to get moving. This was the second day and the light was already falling from the sky. Cassidy had to get the Heart. Get the Heart and get back to her world or she might be stuck in this dead world forever. She heaved a heavy sigh. *You'd think you'd get better at this over time?*

"So," she said, "how are you going to do that?"

Don't forget about Fletcher.

"No, I won't." Cassidy struggled to her feet (which now burned and flared with a sharp pain).

What are you going to do?

"Get Fletcher. Get the Heart. Get home." Cassidy limped out of the alley and forced herself to keep moving in the general direction of Fletcher's base. She stopped, leaning one hand on the rough brick of the building to her right, and she nodded to herself.

"Wait. First, I'll get reinforcements."

And not the kind that are only looking for your dead body.

"Then, with their help, I'll get Fletcher. Help Fletcher dispose of Beckett. Get the heart. Then, get back home. How's that?" Cassidy said and stumbled forward.

***

She was lost. The night had fallen sooner than she had anticipated (was that another quirk of this New York that wasn't her New York?). Cassidy was sure that she was headed in the right direction and moving toward the freeway they'd entered this part of the city through. Even so, she couldn't find a freeway, or anything that looked like it. There were no ramps, no openings, nothing. Just block after block of abandoned buildings.

Cassidy's muscles were begging her to give them a break. They rippled unbidden and seemed on the verge of giving up the game whether Cassidy allowed them to do so or not. She cursed. She had to find shelter. She needed the rest, though she certainly didn't want to imagine what her muscles would feel like in the morning. Another curse was spat into the open air.

Eventually she came across an old building, not quite a brownstone, but close enough. Three in a row actually, but the one she eyed didn't have the door beat in, and the door handle and lock were where they were supposed to be.

Cassidy opened the door with as much caution as her shaking muscles would allow her and poked her head in. It was dark. The interior was completely shielded from the dull light of the moon and stars. The air was dry and had the sour odour of dust and neglect. If someone had been using this place as a shelter it was a long time ago.

Her muscles gave her enough leeway to drag herself in through the entrance and close the door before she collapsed to her knees. It was a bittersweet relief that washed over her. She wanted to just lie where she'd fallen. She wanted to lie there and sleep and forget about her weary muscles and guns and dead worlds and no cellphones.

Mustering all her will and remaining strength, she managed to crawl into the living area of the little house and into a corner that faced the entrance way. She couldn't be sure that no one followed her, or that they couldn't track her stumbling, erratic trek into a strange part of this unknown New York. Cassidy needed to be prepared in case someone tried to surprise her in the middle of the night.

With her head leaning against the wall behind her she stared at the door, her mind racing despite the exhaustion of her body. How could she be certain there weren't other factions roaming the deserted city? Fletcher had mentioned that most people had been moved to farmland to make a living, but his group was able to escape that life.

Who's to say that another group didn't as well?

Could there be another group of freedom fighters, or a band of thieves looking to survive off the suffering of other people?

And what would they do with a bone-tired archaeologist from another world with nothing more than a cheap EMF and a collapsible shovel?

"Doesn't matter, I'll make them eat it if they aren't friendly," she said with a weak swat towards her satchel.

She nodded to herself then and fought back an unbidden laugh. All she needed to do was sit in the dark. They'd miss her at a cursory glance, and by the time they got around to really studying the space, she'd be awake and ready for them. She'd done it before, she'd be able to do it again.

Were you this tired back then?

"Yes, I was exhausted." She cleared her throat. Anyway, there was nothing more that she could do about it now. She needed to sleep, she needed to rest. When the daylight reappeared, she'd find the freeway, get her backup, and finish all this. She'd be back home before supper time.

This time she did laugh as her eyelids closed over her dry, strained eyes and she crossed over into a deep, uninterrupted sleep. Never aware that she was being watched, and watched closely.

CHAPTER EIGHT

When Cassidy woke, the reality of her night came back to her in bits and pieces. She took a minute and confirmed that she felt fine, all things considered, and, with great effort, stretched. The aches and pains of the previous day's activity fell on her like a leaden weight. She cried out as her limbs fought against her attempts to move and pulled back, tight. Cassidy could feel her calf muscles dance on the verge of a cramp.

"No, no, no..." she said through gritted teeth and somehow managed to pull her legs back and massage them into a semblance of relaxation.

"That's it. Gym. As soon as I'm done this, I'm signing up for the gym," she said with a sigh and fell back against the wall again.

"Jim? No, I'm Argyle," the voice came from another room.

Cassidy watched as a shadow of a figure crept around the doorway from the next room over. Its legs were long and spindly, bunched up as it crawled into her room. Its hands were flat on the floor and pulled it forward. Its long fingernails scraped over the laminate flooring as it went.

She reached for her shovel, but her satchel wasn't by her side.

Did I take it off, she thought as she fixed herself to be squared up with the creature that had just made its way into her space.

Despite her still sleep addled mind protesting against it, the creature was most certainly a human. She didn't have to push far past her initial fright to see it. Legs, arms, head – all where they were supposed to be. And then there were the creature's eyes. Bright white, save the small brown iris that wouldn't move from her.

"Some call me the Rat," the creature said and pulled out a football helmet to place in the centre of the room. "But I'm Argyle. Always have been, always will be." He shambled over and sat on the helmet, Green Bay Packers judging by the colours. He drew his knees to his chest and crossed his arms over them, still studying her.

"Where…"

"Argyle owns the house. Owns this street, this block, this city." He gestured with both hands, "It's Argyle's."

"Were you here when I showed up last night?" Cassidy said and fought to keep the anger from her voice.

"Oh yes, Argyle watched you come in. He watched you crawl to that corner and watched you fall asleep. You slept well, yes?"

Not if I knew some creep was watching me, Cassidy thought. She could feel the ache in her back and legs begin anew, her shock subsiding. She wanted to sit down again, to give herself a minute to get used to the idea of stretching out her tensed muscles. The thought of sliding down the corner to sit again crossed her mind, but it was soon overridden with another darker image. A premonition of Argyle, as quick and agile as a spider, scuttling across the space between them and on her – all limbs and teeth. Cassidy shot a quick glance at the man's mouth, it was a red slash in the early morning darkness. She shuddered.

"Argyle, where is my bag?" Cassidy tried to ignore the pain and stood away from the wall with her shoulders squared and back; ready.

Argyle squinted at her, his eyes suspicious. He turned his torso to the side and tried to keep it out of sight. "Argyle doesn't know anything about a bag," he said, yellowed teeth bared some.

Cassidy wanted to curse and pounce on him, beat him until he admitted he had her satchel, but she held herself steady. There was something in Argyle's eyes that told her there was another way. Something in the way he looked at her.

"Argyle," she said and put her fists on her hips, "are you lying to me?"

One of his lips curled back over his yellowed teeth in a sneer, "No."

"Argyle, this isn't how you treat guests, is it?"

His stance faltered some and he turned back towards Cassidy, sulking.

"Taking someone's things is an awful lot like something a rat would do. You're not a rat are you?"

"I'm Argyle. I always have been, always will be," he said and puffed out his chest.

"That's right," Cassidy said through a forced smile, "so where are my things Argyle?"

He pouted some, but he pulled her satchel out of his

long, grey coat and handed it to her. His eyes finally left her face. They turned to the ground.

"Thanks, I appreciate that," Cassidy fought the urge to check inside the bag to make sure everything was there.

That might be pushing my luck a bit, she thought and slung the pack over her shoulder.

"You have good tech in there," Argyle said. His eyes fluttering between her face and the ground. "I bet Beckett really likes you. Do you work for Beckett?"

"No," she said cautiously. Perhaps this was the grey coat's version of a bloodhound. Cassidy fought a sneer from appearing on her own face.

"Good," Argyle said with a sigh. "Argyle doesn't either. I just," he shifted his eyes to the left and right, "I just borrowed this coat." He opened the coat as if it relieved him of all implications.

"Do they like you much, Argyle?" Cassidy had the feeling that she already knew the answer to this, but wanted to keep him talking.

"Oh no, Beckett does not like Argyle. His men try to hurt me, to take my things. Beckett is just jealous. He thinks he's the Lord of this city, but it is Argyle's city. Argyle is… Argyle is king!"

"Well, Argyle, Beckett doesn't like me much right now either. But he has something of mine, and I need to get it back."

"Yes? Yes, what is it Beckett has of yours?" Argyle skittered a little closer to her, leaving the helmet behind. Cassidy stepped back into the wall.

"Well… he has something called the Digital Heart, have you ever heard of that?"

Argyle rubbed his chin and scratched his head. "No, Argyle hasn't heard of a Digital Heart. A heart," he thumped his chest, "but not a Digital Heart. What is it?"

"Oh it's just this little thing, but it's important to me. Very important."

Argyle nodded his head.

"He also has a friend of mine. I need to save him."

"A friend?" Argyle shook his head. "Beckett doesn't like friends. He doesn't like keeping them for long."

"Do you know where he would be?" Cassidy heard the panic slip into her voice, but that couldn't be helped. Not now.

"Beckett keeps them close, do you know where Beckett lives?"

"The squat hotel with the cameras."

"Yes, yes. Your friend will be there. Argyle is sure of it."

Cassidy held her breath for a long moment. She had wanted to get back-up, to get Fletcher's small rebellion to come to her aid, storm Beckett's so-called castle, and rescue Fletcher. Argyle could probably point her in the right direction, and get her started on the trek back to Fletcher's home base. That would take most of the day, and even then would anyone even be there? They had daily scouting trips planned, and Fletcher wouldn't be missed for another day. There'd be no reason to halt their original plans. Even if everything went perfectly and they were all there, ready to go when she arrived, would they believe her? They didn't know her, and Fletcher had treated her like an enemy the minute he met her. Would they be any different, especially if she returned saying that Fletcher was captured? They'd probably blame her for it. By the time she could convince them otherwise, her three days would be up and Fletcher would be dead. There just wasn't enough time.

"Argyle," Cassidy spoke slowly, "could you show me where Beckett lives? I've forgotten the way."

***

Before noon they left the house. Argyle wanted some assurances and some of her tech. After a brief discussion, he settled for the EMF reader and the promise that he didn't have to set foot inside Beckett's building.

The skittering creature Cassidy had associated with Argyle transformed as they exited onto the street. In the open space, Argyle stretched out his legs, a series of pops and cracks sounded in opposition. Arms stretched toward the sky, he stood almost seven feet tall. It took Cassidy a moment to adjust to the sudden, and unexpected, change. She had students in her class, basketball players mostly, who were six foot seven, six foot eight, but Argyle put them to shame. His fingers were long and lean and highlighted by long, often curved, fingernails. Through the initial shock of Argyle at his full forbearance, Cassidy could only focus on how glad she was that she didn't choose to tangle with him.

"Come," Argyle's voice was hushed, his restless eyes constant as they roamed the buildings that surrounded them.

Cassidy could vaguely remember her surroundings from the night before, but the path Argyle was leading her over seemed more familiar than not. The brownstones

they had left were an oddity of that neighbourhood, surrounded by large grey concrete monoliths that parted
only in their middle for doors and spotted with windows.
When Cassidy looked up to the sky, a lone curtain seemed
to blow out into the wind like a flag at half mast. It was
that image, the lone curtain, that made her thankful for
choosing Argyle's brownstone. Images of creatures far
worse than Argyle crawling through that building floated
up from her imagination. Creatures with unseeing red
eyes, stripped to the waist, and foam dripping from their
fang-like teeth. She shuddered and hurried after Argyle.

Their pace was slow, but constant. Argyle sniffed at
the air, cocked his ear to some distant sound Cassidy had
no hope of hearing, and poked through debris as if it were
some sort of treasure trove – or a dead body he was ensur-
ing was properly deceased. He halted their advance many
times, and scurried off on all fours, often reappearing from
a high ledge or window, his face grim and mouth set in a
frown. Cassidy had spent more than her fair share of time
dealing with paranoid sherpas, self-conscious trackers,
and overzealous hunters, so she was aware of what Argyle
was doing – at least she thought so. The poor fear-addled
man was checking for traps, for spies, and for anything
that would give away their position. He was cautious, but
perhaps that was what living the life of a scavenger in this
world was painted with: caution. Cassidy shrugged, he
knew the way and she didn't, she had little choice but to
allow him his extended rituals.

It was well after midday before they entered an area of
the city that Cassidy had some recollection of. It was the
freeway Fletcher had led her through.

"That's where I came from," Cassidy said pointing out the freeway exit to Argyle. She didn't quite know why she said it and certainly didn't understand why she had to say it to Argyle.

You don't want him to think you're stupid. That you're a stupid, lost little girl that needs his help.

That could be, she thought and felt a frown deepen on her face. For Argyle's part, he just shrugged and went back to sniffing the air.

***

The first arrow struck the ground in front of them. Cassidy's recollection had been growing the further they ventured into the city, and she felt a wave of relief when they reached the buildings that she and Fletcher had explored before the ambush. She was about to mention this to Argyle when he yelped and skittered backwards into the shade of an alleyway. The arrow struck a moment after and sent Cassidy backpedalling into the alley with Argyle.

"That was sooner than expected," Cassidy said, trying to look around the edge of the building to see where the archer was.

"Beckett moves positions. Especially when he's suspicious." Argyle growled and studied the building they were leaning against.

"Makes sense. I was only here yesterday," Cassidy massaged her sore tricep muscles.

Argyle grunted and stretched up, grabbing the ledge of a window that Cassidy hadn't noticed until she heard Argyle's fingernails scratch across it. With one quick pull he was up, his long legs hanging briefly in midair over her head.

"Come," he said, his wild face appeared and he slithered one long arm down for her.

An arrow cracked against the asphalt road and Cassidy could hear the shouts of men getting closer and closer. She jumped up and grasped Argyle's wrist, his long fingers wrapped around hers in return. The feel of his thin fingers and their too long nails caused a ripple of disgust to walk up and down her spine.

Argyle dragged her into another dark room. She wasn't surprised. The gloomy light from the overcast sky tried to pierce the darkness in that room, but it was of little use. Cassidy pulled her hand away from Argyle, his bright white eyes seemed to be the only thing she could see in the gloom and moved further away from the window. She tripped over something and fell on her ass. The sudden jolt of pain set all her muscles to aching again as if her body was one big cramp. Cassidy stifled a scream. She was really starting to hate this world and its lack of electricity.

She reached around and pulled up what she had tripped over. A wooden baseball bat. She ran her hand over its length, feeling the smooth surface spotted with dry spots where the lacquer had been worn away.

"Wait, they're…," she started, but was cut off by a sudden howl that came from the door as it was kicked open.

A lone silhouette burst into the room with a metal bar or baton raised above its head. Cassidy couldn't make out the minute details, but they had on a grey jacket.

Cassidy started to rise to meet the man, the baseball

bat in her hands and ready to club him about the knees, but, again, she was cut off -- this time by Argyle. A loud, screech went up from her spindly guide and he threw himself upon the attacker, not giving him enough time to bring down his weapon.

She faltered. Argyle had his arms and legs wrapped around the man, his face was at his neck and just under the screams of the attacker, Cassidy thought she could hear a chewing or slurping sound. Her stomach wavered and she leaned on the open window, the fresh air suddenly very welcome.

There was yelling outside and a sudden crash from somewhere not too far below her. *The door,* she thought. *They're coming.*

Cassidy didn't spare a glance at Argyle and the fallen grey coat; she wasn't sure that her stomach could've handled it anyway. She pushed passed them into a stairwell, even darker than the room she had just left. Noises drifted up from the floor below: muffled conversations, stomping of feet.

"They don't know we're here," Argyle poked his head through the doorway and Cassidy nearly screamed. What little light there was reflected from Argyle's too white eyes, and she was glad for it. There was a slick sheen on his face and chin, black in the near dark, that she knew she didn't want a clearer image of. "They're just looking. More are in the street."

Yes, Cassidy thought, that had some sense to it. They couldn't find them in the alley, so they'd check the buildings. They hadn't expected Argyle to be so tall, so they didn't figure anyone would be on the second floor, only on the first. Keep quiet, don't move, she thought and repeated it as a mantra. Keep quiet, don't move.

Easier said than done, she thought, steeling herself to return to the first room. The room with Argyle in it. The room with Argyle's victim. She hesitated at the doorway, cocked her ear to the noise on the first floor again. It was quieter already. Some, if not all of them had moved out, likely exploring other buildings. Hunting. They'd have to stay away from the windows.

She heard another familiar sound. Cassidy was just about to strengthen her efforts to return to the room with Argyle when the low pitch tickled her ear. It wasn't something she had yet heard in this world, and she'd become so accustomed to the pervading silence that entombed this version of New York that she couldn't place it at first. It was loud. Even at a distance it was loud. Like the roar of some wild animal echoing over the vast dead wasteland. But that wasn't it. Then it roared again.

Cassidy's eyes popped open wide and she turned towards the blackness that contained Argyle. "Is that a car?"

Though she couldn't see him do it, Cassidy knew that Argyle was nodding. "Beckett is moving."

"What the hell does that mean?"

"He has many homes in Argyle's city," said Argyle's disembodied voice. "Many homes, many hiding places." That last word he drew out with a long 's' sound.

Cassidy she ran up over the stairs. If there was a car running in this version of New York, she had to see it.

CHAPTER NINE

She took the stairs two at a time, her throbbing muscles an afterthought as Cassidy pushed her way up one floor after another. Her footsteps sounded like small explosions that boomed through the building, though she paid little heed to them. The only sound that she focused on was the roar of the engine as it got closer and closer.

Far too loud to be a Toyota Tercel, Cassidy thought, turning the corner on another set of stairs. Has a lot of rumble to it, maybe a truck or a suped up Mustang? Better yet, a Camaro.

Cassidy's mind rolled over the possibilities as she made her way up to another level still, but there was something else nagging at her. Something Argyle had said.

Cassidy came to the top of the stairs. There was a metal door to her right, a large number 8 stencilled on it next to a window that had what looked like chicken wire running through the panes. Not giving herself enough time to take a deep breath, she pulled open the door and ran into the room, her eyes searching for the nearest window, or exit. She had to see the car.

She busted through an office door and tossed a chair

to the floor to clear her path to a dust-ridden, dirty window. She was in luck. With a flick of the lock and a twist of the handle, Cassidy was out on a small metal balcony, a cool breeze blowing her hair across her eyes.

The rumble of the engine grew louder as it got closer, a roar that was interrupted by a harsh clanking noise. "Gear change," Cassidy muttered, and placed her hand over her eyes to stop the sun from interrupting her view. Plumes of black smoke appeared in the sky not far off, and another belch of gear changing as it pushed itself forward. Diesel, Cassidy thought, a truck.

It was more than a truck that turned a corner and pulled into view. A tractor trailer pulled into view; its roar not silenced by the turn into the main drag. The truck itself was a shining red, two chrome exhaust shafts climbed up behind the doors and continued to unfurl black plumes into the air. The sun struck the windshield and hid the driver behind its glare as the trailer behind it continued to pull itself into view.

Cassidy thought the sight of the truck, of such a familiar object, accompanied by its commonplace, if unwavering sound, would shake the unnerving emptiness that she felt in this dead world. She thought that it might make her feel more comfortable, even at ease. It didn't. The sight of the truck was like a stone sinking in her stomach. The earth-shaking noise made her flinch, and she suddenly had the urge to hide away from the smoke-spewing, mechanical beast that was about to thunder toward her.

Try as she might to pull away, to flee back through the window, something continued to draw her towards the truck. Was it something Argyle said?

"Beckett is moving," whispered in her mind. Cassidy turned to see if Argyle had crept up behind her, but the window was empty.

He has many homes… many homes, many hiding places.

Cassidy strained her eyes trying to see the driver, why were Argyle's words sticking with her?

The Heart! If Beckett was moving, he would be taking the Heart with him.

"True," Cassidy said and bit her lip, but there was something else. Something on the tip of her tongue.

Besides, what was she going to do, jump on the trailer and hitch a ride to his new hideout, ambush a small army of armed men, just because Gamgee saw some graffiti? Not a chance. It would make more sense to head home, tell Gamgee about what she found. Tell him about the dead world, the eerie facsimile of New York, about the make-shift feudal government, and about Fletcher's freedom fighters. Let Gamgee decide if it was worth it.

Fletcher.

Cassidy cursed herself. Fletcher was in that truck. He was on that trailer.

"Stupid, stupid, stupid," Cassidy said and paced the small balcony. Fletcher was an asshole of the first degree but leaving him to Beckett now was as good as leaving him alone in the first place. Besides, coming back here was about helping Fletcher, not the Digital Heart. Right?

He might be dead. Or Beckett might have left him behind, travel light and all that.

"Does he look like he's travelling light?" Cassidy waved a hand toward the eighteen-wheeler that rolled her way.

Good point.

"Thank you," Cassidy said and climbed over the railing in front of her.

Below her she could see a similar balcony to the one she'd just left. She eased herself down and swung into it, a loud clang resounding as she landed. There were shouts from below, but she didn't have time to worry about that. She repeated the process and moved to a lower balcony.

Let me figure this out, she thought and moved down to another level. *An average tractor trailer is about fourteen feet high. Each storey in a building is about ten feet high.*

Another level.

"So," she said out loud between gulping breaths, "second story will be about twenty feet high, right?" She stopped and looked for the truck. It had completed its laborious turn and was chugging straight for her. It was picking up speed.

"Or, would the balcony of the third floor be at twenty feet and the ceiling of the third floor be thirty feet?" She cursed. "What bloody storey am I on anyway?"

It didn't matter. The truck was picking up the speed that it had lost in the turn but getting faster and faster. If she was going to do this, she had to do it now.

She climbed over the railing. *The last railing I'll be climbing over*, she told herself. Making sure her heels were able to fit between the bars easily; she reached her arms back to hold the railing. The position had the strange benefit of stretching out some of the aches and pains that she had managed to push out of her mind for a moment or two. It felt good.

The truck blared its horn as it passed underneath her,

and the sound almost made her lose her grip. Cassidy chuckled and watched as the red truck moved from her sight and the large white trailer filled her view.

"Am I still too high up?" she managed before yelling a loud litany of curses and letting herself fall on the trailer. *This is going to hurt,* she managed to think before she slammed into the trailer and everything went fuzzy.

CHAPTER TEN

The trailer top was slick. Cassidy slapped at the surface and willed her palms to grip tight. She cursed when they failed to do so. Cassidy flailed and slid towards the edge. She kicked her boots out, the thick rubber soles tried to do their job but couldn't catch and wouldn't hold.

"Idiot," Cassidy growled. "You're an idiot."

With one more big effort she pushed herself up on her knees and lodged a boot along the slightly raised edge of the trailer to slow her momentum. She took advantage of her borrowed time and wiped her hands on her pants. She couldn't stretch across the width of the trailer to grab a hold of the other side while her boots lodged where it was for a foothold.

So, it's either my hands or my feet, Cassidy thought.

Cassidy pushed off the small edge and grabbed a hold of the side, her hands latched onto the small outcropping. Her body tried to roll to the side and her arms strained against the momentum to keep her in place. With another grunt she sprawled her legs out so that the sides of her boots connected with the trailer top. With more area coverage the rubber grips kept her from moving. With an extra effort she pulled herself up, her biceps tight and pain-ful with her elbows tight to her ribs.

She was secure enough, her hips moving with the motion of the truck to keep her in place. Everything hurt but she held on, her fingers numbing.

Turning her head towards the building she'd leapt from Cassidy caught a glimpse of the bright white eyes of Argyle staring from an open window. His bright red gash of a mouth agape as he watched the truck go, a grimace of pain or sadness painting it.

"I hope you enjoy the EMF buddy," Cassidy grunted and focused on making sure she didn't fall off the speeding truck.

***

"Shut up and move," a gruff voice came from some-where below. Cassidy slid herself closer to the end of the trailer.

The trailer had backed up to a derelict building about three stories high. Whatever colour it had been painted in the past was lost to the years and the only colour that attracted any attention was the rust that was smeared across the building's surface. The truck pulled up to a loading area complete with a tattered awning that, despite being completely shredded, managed to block Cassidy's view. With a silent curse she manoeuvred herself around just to get a glimpse of what was happening.

"Move it," the voice came again, followed by the sound of a hard shove that sent someone scrambling. A flash of grey appeared through the torn cloth of the awning; the back of a grey hat, brown hair crawling from underneath it. Another head passed under the hole a little too quickly to get a clear picture of anything but a blur.

Was that Fletcher's ill-fitting stocking cap? Cassidy didn't want to speculate on it. She had to believe he was alive and that she was able to help him.

A flash of a bald head followed the blur into the building. Cassidy pushed herself out of sight, the loud chunk sound of metal bending and popping back into shape rose from underneath her and she froze, a curse ready on the tip of her tongue.

The shuffling of feet stopped, a pregnant silence fell that caused Cassidy to hold her breath and hug tighter into the trailer's roof. A cough broke the silence, but the tension only increased. Cassidy could feel her heart beat against her chest and she had a momentary fear that the thudding might beat a tattoo on the top of the trailer and reveal her position.

A door closed and the tension disappeared. Cassidy poked her head over the edge of the trailer once more. There was no movement, no sense of anyone out there except her, and the brief elation disguised as relief that allowed her to breath again in long, deep sighs.

After another ten minutes of waiting, silent with her cheek resting on the cool trailer's surface, Cassidy climbed down to rest her feet on the solid ground.

"Still got my sea legs," she said, one hand on the trailer to steady her as she peered around the back. The large metal doors under that awning were shut and there was no apparent handle on their dented surface. The trailer door was left open, its plywood floors empty save for some garbage strewn about.

"They made quick work of it," she said studying the water stains and dirt encrusted boot prints. She tried to count the differing boot treads, but they crossed over each other too much, and she was never good at tracking live people. Give her a footprint preserved in a fossilized lakebed or volcanic ash and she'd follow them all the way to their end. Tracks of living people were just too unpredictable.

"There's only one thing for it," Cassidy said and moved up the three concrete steps to the doors. Her legs still wobbled, and she had to force herself to walk without a limp. Pain crackled up her legs to her hips, but it was manageable. For now.

The doors were steel, heavy and thick. A solitary deadbolt receptacle marred the face of the right-hand door and it looked new. Well, newer than the rest of the building anyway, Cassidy thought. Pockmarks of rust and corrosion were smattered about the otherwise shiny surface.

"It has to be locked," Cassidy whispered and tried to wedge her fingers under the lip of the door. It opened with a gentle pull; the setting sun cast an orange light into the shade of the building's interior.

Cassidy grabbed her shovel from her bag and moved into the building, her eyes on every corner.

The shade disappeared as Cassidy walked into the building. The light was artificial, a throbbing unnatural yellow that buzzed into desperate life. The fluorescents stung her eyes, and Cassidy put one hand over her brow to tone it down. She'd only been away from the electrical world for three days and already man-made light was giving her trouble. For someone like Fletcher, who hadn't experienced that sort of light in years, it must have been torture.

The door closed behind her with a subtle click. With her shovel cocked back and ready to strike, Cassidy moved further into the room. It was a storage bay, aging and decrepit boxes still hugged into the walls, their wares long since removed or stolen. A counter greeted her about halfway into the room, an old cash register stood a silent guard, its drawer left open like some ancient robot with its tongue torn from its own jaws. The cash was long gone.

Cheap tiled floors matched the tiles in the dropped ceiling above, and large, steel shelving units cut across the remainder of the room. Boxes and filth lined them, untouched and covered in a thick layer of dust. The light had stopped working over the empty shelves and Cassidy plunged into darkness towards a sliver of light that may have been the outline of a door.

The next room was plagued by offices, a haphazard few of the fluorescent lights above painted a trail through the open space. The office doors were ajar, ransacked within, their desks and chairs overturned, broken. Cassidy moved on, cautious of each shadowy entrance, hoping an arrow or crossbow bolt wouldn't come at her from a dark corner.

A shuffling sound brought her to a halt, the far-off echoes of a casual conversation carried to her from above. Cassidy shuffled into an office with little debris blocking its entrance directly to her right. Shovel still at the ready, she waited.

"Not sure why we had to move again," a voice said as its owner approached. "They didn't find anything, and it was only the girl."

"And the Rat, don't forget about him," said another voice, younger than the first. "That girl you're talking about claimed to be a garbagemancer and she gave Harrison a nasty bump on his bald head."

"She did at that," the first voice said, stifling a chuckle. "Still, hard to believe there's any more garbagemancers out there. And the Rat, well, he'd be as fine with a joint of meat and some trinkets as anything else."

The grey coats passed by Cassidy's hiding place, her back pushed against the wall while her head strained to maintain her view on them. She held her breath.

"Well, garbagemancer or not, she had a working piece of tech. If those, what does Beckett call them, the rebels? If the rebels have working tech, Beckett is going to want to know. He'll get it out of the other one. No problem."

Another laugh.

"Especially with Harrison in such a foul mood. Poor fella will wish he was dead before too long."

Laughter followed them out of the room.

It was another minute before Cassidy allowed herself to take another breath. The silence had resumed outside of the office, and she stepped into it willingly. Her heart pounded in her chest and her grip tightened on her shovel. It seemed to her that Fletcher and the Digital Heart would be in close vicinity to one another. With another deep breath, Cassidy girded herself to climb the stairs. It was a steep, narrow stairwell; the yellow painted walls were sloughing off chipped paint and was much too close to her shoulders. Her shovel's blade scraped along the wall for a split-second, sending a shriek of metal against concrete through the small area and sent paint chips floating to the floor. Yellow snow flakes dusted the ground.

Cassidy fought her instincts, pushed her way through the door at the top of the stairs and hurried away from the stairway. The icy fingers of yellow paint reached out to her, beckoned to her as the door swung shut behind her.

This level of the building had a more open floor plan, with the immediate area in front of her devoid of anything. The torn linoleum floor was empty, scuff marks and long-standing dents from furniture that had once littered it still stood as a reminder of life before everything went to ground. The room was divided by a wall, one door at its centre.

Cassidy moved forward and leaned on the wall next to the door. Playing a slow game, she placed her ear to the door.

CHAPTER ELEVEN

Nothing.

Whatever was on the other side of that door, she couldn't hear it.

Her hand glided over the brass doorknob, it rattled at her touch and she jumped back as if she'd laid a hand on a hot stove. She sighed.

"Come on Cassidy," she said and wiped the sweat from her palms, "no pain, no gain." With a grimace she pushed open the door.

"Crap," Cassidy stared into the eyes of Baldy, or Harrison, as he leaned over the bound form of Fletcher, his head drooped to his chest.

Harrison's eyes burned, his face clenched like a fist. Free of his grey coat, wearing only a white tank top spattered with blood, Cassidy could see his thickly corded arms mapped with scars and thick, black hair. Black leather gloves adorned his hands, which were filled with Fletcher's shirt, in mid-throttle.

"Howdy," Cassidy said with a small wave. "Am I interrupting something?"

Harrison dropped Fletcher and stood at his full height.

It was only then, as the bald man's head caught the light did Cassidy notice the large bump that protruded from Harrison's forehead, and the purple bruise bloomed around his eye.

Everything that came next happened in slow motion. Harrison adjusted his gloves, wiggled his fingers into place, a smug grin grew under his thick moustache. He bolted forward, his arms pumping with purpose, his legs a blur, his eyes on Cassidy.

Cassidy's instincts took over. She spun away from the charge with a gasp and gave herself some space and time to think. Harrison growled and spun on her, his feet skidded to a stop casting off dust in light clouds.

He charged again, his teeth clenched and the glint of saliva running down his chin. A curse on her tongue, Cassidy was ready for him. Legs braced, she took a deep breath and raised her shovel.

As he got closer Cassidy feinted with a swing aimed at his face. Harrison reacted, brought himself to a stop and covered his face with one hand, the other reaching out as if to grab the shovel.

A smile lit on Cassidy's face and she dropped her swing downward. The flat part of the shovel blade slammed into one of Harrison's knees, emphasized by a loud popping sound. The effect was immediate. Harrison cried out in surprise and agony as he dropped to the floor holding his leg and rolling around on his back.

Cassidy stood back, dropped her shovel to the ground. She could still feel the vibration of the impact in the palms of her hands.

"Finish it," Fletcher coughed from behind her. He

wasn't in good shape. The bridge of his nose sported a thick slash and blood (both dried and fresh) had cascaded down around either side of his nose and into his beard. One of his eyes was swollen shut, red and angry. The opposite cheek was purple with the outline of fingers bruised there. His mouth was the worst. His lips had been smashed into his teeth so often that they were twice their usual size, cracked, bleeding. A mixture of spit and blood dripped down his chin.

"What?" Cassidy said hurrying to untie Fletcher, ignoring the groans of pain that Harrison's screams had devolved into.

"Kill him," Fletcher fell forward out of his chair, landing on his hands and knees. He spat a glob of blood to the side.

Cassidy rushed to his side and helped him up. "He's down. He can't do anything right now. It's safe for us…"

"Not if he calls out for help, or if he gets to his…" Fletcher pushed Cassidy out of the way and launched himself toward the small table that was next to his chair. His fumbling hands struck the table and knocked it to the floor, instruments sliding further into the room. A gun slid with them. It was a Glock, dark as a black hole, that drew their eyes. The room went silent, as if it was holding a breath.

Fletcher's eyes locked with Cassidy's and they both scrambled forward to grab the gun. Fletcher growled, his face red, his expression livid. Cassidy, for her part, didn't know why they were fighting over the gun, not really. Her gut though, it screamed at her to grab it, that it was important for her to reach it before Fletcher or Harrison could.

Crawling over each other, they fought. An elbow thrown here, a fist looped to the midsection there, a shoe scraped over shin. Fletcher was more savage than Cassidy and he lashed out with tooth and nail. Cassidy was fresher, her injuries much more subdued than Fletcher's own, and her strength held. She was winning.

Her hand stretched out so that her fingertips grazed the butt of the gun, but Cassidy was stopped short. Fletcher had his hand wrapped around her belt and was pulling her back. She looked back at his ruined face and saw a stinging hatred in his one open eye. With her leg cocked, she jammed her foot into his stomach and pushed off.

Cassidy could see her hand's shadow over the gun; she had it.

"I'll take that," a calm, high pitched voice said. A thin hand scooped up the gun and pointed it down at Fletcher and Cassidy, "I think you're both here for me."

Fletcher, still sprawled on top of her, groaned and released her. Cassidy pushed away from him and looked up at the figure before her. Toothpick thin legs extended out of maroon slippers, faux fur tickling at his ankles. A too short bathrobe, maroon to match the slippers, clutched eagerly around his waist, the same faux fur poked out of the sleeves to grip to the man's skeletal elbows. Sticking out of the robe on a pencil thin neck, a globule of a head with sunken eyes and pointing jaw with a wisp of a goatee covering it. Long, golden brown hair that was piled high in a self-important man-bun.

"Beckett?" Cassidy's face twitched with a grin.

"At your service," Beckett said and did a little bow, his hair flopped forward with his head. The gun didn't waver in his hand.

"I suppose you're this one's partner then?" Beckett jabbed the barrel of the gun towards Fletcher. "The one that got away." He rolled his eyes and paced back and forth in front of them. He actively refrained from looking at Harrison, whose groans had resumed.

"I hope you know that you ruined a perfectly cushy and comfortable lair. This," Beckett waved his free hand around the room, "this... warehouse is a plan b. Plan c! Never had I expected to be imprisoned here, not when the hotel had everything that I needed. Follow me," he beckoned with the gun and backed into another room, his grey eyes never moving from Cassidy or Fletcher.

They followed him into what turned out to be little more than a kitchenette. Linoleum floor with some long-faded pattern and speckled with some ancient grey paint that had been painted over with the pale yellow that now adorned the walls. In one corner of the room was a small table covered in all sorts of kitchen accoutrements, the necessities of any workplace break room: coffee maker, toaster oven, microwave. Each appliance dirty under several years' worth of dust. An electric tea kettle was the only thing in the room clearly spotless. It sat on the counter of the kitchenette next to a single tub sink, its cord dangling toward the shabby flooring.

"Harrison," Beckett called, leaning on the counter, a smile creeping slowly over his bulbous lips. "Do you want tea, darling?" He switched the gun to his left hand, his eyes still focused on Cassidy and Fletcher as they stumbled to a halt just inside the door.

With a nod to himself, Beckett reached his free hand

out and touched the base of the electric kettle. A subtle twitch came over his face, and he took two long blinks, his eyes rolled and fell back onto his prisoners.

To Cassidy's surprise, the orange light on the base of the kettle flickered to life.

"Come now," Beckett said, a less subtle grin stretching across his mouth, "you've seen me drive a truck, and a little tea kettle is more shocking to you?" He chortled, and steam began to rise from the kettle's spout.

"Well, it's just that, uh," Cassidy could feel her cheeks flush, "I didn't really think about the truck. This is, well, different." She pointed to the neglected cord, its three pronged plug swaying in front of the counter.

"More of a visual, eh?" Beckett shot a quick look at the kettle, steam rising quickly from it now. "Be a dear, get me a cup from that cupboard," he indicated the cupboard furthest away from him, the gun waving her toward it.

"Thank you," Beckett said when Cassidy had a tea cup set on the counter in front of her. "Now, just in front of you, in the canister, pull out a tea bag and place it in the cup."

Cassidy gripped the canister in her hands and pulled it forward. It was an old-fashioned yellow with white highlights depicting a tea kettle, a dish, and a mug that smattered itself into some out of joint pattern. The lid was held shut by two latches on either side. She hesitated to open it.

"So," she said, playing with the first latch, "how did you, of all people, manage to become a garbagemancer?"

Beckett made a show of clicking back the hammer of his gun, "That isn't a very polite term, young lady."

Cassidy shot a glance over her shoulder at Fletcher. He was bent over, one arm was laced across his stomach, the other was keeping him steady and standing against the door frame. Fletcher raised an eyebrow and shrugged.

"I'm, uh, sorry," Cassidy said, "but how did you get your powers? I mean, why you and not everyone?"

Beckett removed his hand from the kettle's base and rolled his eyes. "Not very bright, is she?" Beckett said to Fletcher, a frown now diminishing his face.

"I heard it was because of the Digital Heart. Is that true? Do you have the Digital Heart?" Cassidy said and removed the first latch of the tea canister.

"You mean this old thing," Beckett reached into his robe and pulled out a long silver necklace. Fastened on the bottom was something that look like a jump drive, but without the casing or the USB mouth. It was a microchip. "I suppose it doesn't hurt to have something like this lying around. But, to be honest, I had a bit of a natural talent for it." He waved his hand towards the kettle again.

"What is the Digital Heart? It doesn't look like it can do much of anything," Cassidy said and opened the canister. Inside it was a dull, thin metal casting hazy reflections of the light that managed to find its way within. Several tea bags lay at the bottom, awaiting use amongst the remnants of its fallen brothers.

"It's not important," Beckett's voice became serious, his grey eyes hardened. "Let's just say that it gives me and the other Governors a gift. Now, put that god damned tea bag in the cup and bring it here."

Beckett jabbed the gun at her and Cassidy hurried to bring the cup over to him. That done, he shooed her back to stand next to Fletcher.

"I heard that it was the Heart that gave you your pow-ers," Cassidy said and eyed Beckett's necklace. "I just can't figure out how that would work. The Heart is obviously a microchip of some sort, but what's the point of that if you can't read it? You need a computer to read a microchip, and to use a computer you need power."

Beckett frowned, "I have the power," and gestured with his free hand.

"Sure, you do now, but what about before? If you didn't have power how could you use a computer to get the power?" Cassidy could feel Fletcher's stare burn a hole in her back, and she wondered what his thoughts might be on the line of questions she just gave his resident gar-bagemancer.

"You certainly have a lot of time on your hands, com-ing up with stories and implying many things that you wouldn't understand and are just not true," Beckett said, his gun firmly trained on Cassidy. "Ah, Mr. Harrison, I see you've decided to join us. At last."

Baldy pushed his way past Cassidy and Fletcher, and limped his way into the kitchenette, resting his shirtless girth on the edge of the counter on the opposite side of the sink of Beckett. He crossed his arms and seemed to hesitate as to whether he should keep an eye on Cassidy and Fletcher, or pay attention to his boss.

Beckett solved that particular issue for him. Closing his eyes he held out the gun to Harrison, "Please take this and watch our guests while I pour myself some tea." Beck-ett's voice dripped with disdain bordering on disgust. He didn't hold the gun at a distance, pinched between his index finger and thumb like a dirty diaper, but Cassidy wouldn't have been surprised if he had. Harrison took the gun, an ugly sneer crept out from under his moustache as he pointed the business end at Cassidy and Fletcher.

"Thank you," Beckett said and poured his tea.

Then, with an ear-splitting bang, the world turned upside down.

CHAPTER TWELVE

The explosion shook the building and threw Cassidy to the floor. Judging by the thud she heard behind her, Fletcher had fallen as well.

Both Harrison and Beckett were thrown off guard and sprawled to the floor. Harrison still had his hand wrapped around the gun. Cassidy wasn't surprised; he wouldn't chance letting that go again.

The shaking stopped as quickly as it had started, the telltale signs of tinnitus buzzed in Cassidy's ears, and by the amount of ear cupping she had witnessed, the others were feeling it too.

"What the hell was that?" Beckett's voice carried to her as if through water; a dull sound that Cassidy could barely hear. Harrison looked at his boss, confusion painting his face as he stuck a finger in one of his ears and shook it around.

Cassidy took her chance. She didn't get herself back to her feet, but instead crouched like a cat and pushed herself from the ground in a leap that bridged the small gap of the kitchenette. She landed on top of Harrison, her two hands gripping his gun hand and pushing it to the floor.

A distant pop sounded as the gun went off, the bullet digging into the worn linoleum.

Harrison bucked underneath her and grabbed a handful of hair with his meaty fist to pull her off. Cassidy kept her weight on the arm with the gun, though she was now forced to look up, her head pulled back and pain lancing through her scalp as her hair ripped away. Finding her bearings wasn't easy with her head pinned back, but she managed to get to a good base, her knees underneath her, and she rammed one into what she hoped was Harrison's crotch. A low grunt escaped from Harrison and he released his hold on Cassidy's hair. She snapped her head forward and let the momentum carry it all the way down until her forehead impacted on Harrison's nose with a sickening crunch she couldn't hear but could certainly feel.

Cassidy felt Harrison release the gun. Her head throbbed and she felt woozy, but she made for the gun. She was slow and it was hard for her to focus. A dull ache grew behind her forehead and her vision blurred with tears.

Her hand grazed the handle of the gun before thin but strong fingers wrapped around her neck from behind. Cassidy reached for her throat, the gun forgotten. She could hear Beckett as a distant echo, though the heat of his breath was hot on her ear.

"What have you done, what have you done?" Beckett's voice was high and strained, his skeletal fingers dug deep into the flesh of Cassidy's neck. She dipped her chin and grabbed for Beckett's hands with her own. His grip was stronger than she imagined for someone with those pale, bony legs.

A red haze flickered at the edge of her vision, her breath came in shallow wheezes that weren't getting the work done. With as much strength as she could muster, Cassidy pushed herself backwards. She could feel the slim frame of Beckett hit the ground and now she was on top of him. His grip hadn't loosened.

With a final gasp, Cassidy gritted her teeth and drove her elbow hard into Beckett's groin. A shriek and an entire body flinch signalled the garbagemancer's loosened grip. Cassidy drove another elbow into his groin and, upon hearing a whine of pain and the harsh exhalation of breath, grabbed at the thin fingers that were now only fumbling at her neck.

She rolled away from Beckett; the man's hands had taken to grabbing at his crotch as he curled into the fetal position. Cassidy held her throat and took short, aching breaths.

A flash passed in the periphery of Cassidy's vision. Without thinking, she turned to face the newcomer; her hand slid over the grip of the gun.

"That's an interesting piece of tech," Argyle said, his mouth a familiar slash of red, his back stooped so that his fingertips grazed the worn linoleum flooring. He looked out at Cassidy through his Green Bay Packers helmet, a smile touching his eyes.

"Argyle?" It hurt Cassidy to talk, her throat hurt, and her voice was hoarse.

"This one's friends," Argyle inclined his head towards Fletcher, "asked me to bring them to Beckett."

"How did you know?" Cassidy said and tried to swallow. She moved towards Fletcher, but hooked the gun in the back of her pants as she went.

"It's my city." Argyle shrugged and moved toward the fallen Harrison and writhing Beckett.

Cassidy moved Fletcher to his back, cringing some from the dried blood that caked his face and the bluish welts that would surely blacken and swell before too long. The ringing in her ears cleared as she stroked Fletcher's hair and tried to coax him into wakefulness. The building was filled with the sounds of fighting; people cursed and screamed and yelped. The twang of arrows and bolts being loosed, the whoosh of a fire starting anew, a short laugh that turned to a harsh cough all flooded Cassidy's recovering ears and attacked her mind.

"Argyle," she said at length, "could you please get someone to help?"

The Rat nodded, his bright eyes tinged with worry as he looked upon her, and then he was gone.

In Argyle's wake, Beckett still clung to his groin with one hand and his whimpers had begun to fade. His other hand was handcuffed to the larger, and still unconscious, Harrison. It wouldn't keep them in place when they were both roused, but Beckett wouldn't be going anywhere while his henchman was out. Beckett knew this. Cassidy had no doubt that he would try to rouse Harrison as soon as his pain subsided. If Argyle wasn't back by then she'd be left alone with them once more. Cassidy put one hand on the pistol grip that poked out of the back of her pants.

"Cassidy?" Fletcher's hand fell on her wrist, his eyes fluttered to life.

"Yeah, I'm here," she smiled and moved his hand to her own.

"What happened?"

"I kicked ass, oh and the rest of your motley crew crashed the party," Cassidy said waving her hand in the air; a far off explosion boomed.

Fletcher tried a smile but settled for a grimace.

"You really weren't kidding about just needing to find this guy?"

Fletcher shook his head. "He's known this would be coming for a while. That's why he kept moving. Potshotted us, reduced our numbers. It could've gone on for a while. We're lucky you came along." He squeezed her hand.

Argyle sauntered back into the room, the small frame of Arturo followed carrying a crossbow nearly his size. An older woman followed after that, someone Cassidy recognized from Fletcher's home base, but whose name escaped her.

"Hey kid," Cassidy said as Arturo took a seat beside her. "Fighting the good fight?" She nodded towards his crossbow, now laid to the side. Arturo gave her a smile, but his focus was on Fletcher.

The old woman took over. From her backpack she produced two first aid kits. One was orange and was labelled as a roadside safety kit, the other was a small white box, the familiar red cross emblazoned on the cover. She removed supplies from each and began to poke and prod at Fletcher.

"I'll need you to give him some space," the woman said and cast a cold stare at Cassidy.

"Wait," Fletcher tightened his grip on Cassidy's hand. "Is it over? Is Beckett dead?"

Cassidy's throat clenched, her chest tightened. Arturo looked beyond them all towards the small counter space. She knew his eyes were running over the prone bodies of Beckett and Harrison. She knew that he was watching to see if their chests still rose and fell with breath.

"No, he's not dead. Neither is Harrison. They're both down and out. They're your prisoners now."

"Harrison..."

"They're worth more alive than dead. You could probably bargain with the other governors, buy yourselves some extra supplies, some more breathing room."

Fletcher patted her hand, nodded his head, "You're right. Of course, you're right. We'll talk more about this later. Please, let Magda get me wrapped up. We'll talk later."

With some effort Fletcher sat up, her hand still in his.

"Thank you, Cassidy. Thank you," Fletcher said and hugged her. He held her tight in his arms and she returned the favour. When they let go, he nodded to her with a smile and she stood and felt a smile of her own paint her face.

It was as she stood that Cassidy realized the gun wasn't hooked in the back of her pants anymore. She reached to feel around, hoping it may have slid further than she meant it to. Her head scanned the floor, afraid it may have fallen out. Then she heard the click.

CHAPTER THIRTEEN

Cassidy looked down the gun barrel. The image was crisp, the gun's black matte colour stood out in a clear and stark contrast to the hazy and unfocused background.

"Who are you, Cassidy?" Fletcher's steady voice rose just above a whisper. "Who are you and what do you want?"

The room around Cassidy was still, silent. It was as though everyone held their breath in anticipation of what was about to come. All eyes were on her, wondering, questioning. How would she answer?

It was the same question that Cassidy was asking herself, and she didn't know. The truth would most likely come across as far-fetched and paint her at best as delusional or worst as a lunatic. Otherwise, she could continue to lie and tell them she was a garbagemancer, but a really nice one. Either way, she didn't have time to explain herself. It was the third day; Gamgee would be closing the portal whether she made it back or not.

"I'm the one who saved your ass," Cassidy said around a growl, the aches and pains of the last few days crashing down on her. "I'm the one that helped you find Beckett in the first place, I'm the one that surfed a damn tractor trailer to find you, and I'm the one that beat the crap out of those two to make sure we're both free."

Cassidy turned to look at Argyle, his helmet now in his hands, "Hell, if I didn't find Argyle and get him involved then you wouldn't have your reinforcements here to blow all this up."

The gun wavered for a second, Fletcher's expression softened with a flash of surprise that left as quickly as it came.

"Why?" Fletcher countered, reaffirming his hold on the pistol.

"Do I need a reason?" Cassidy looked past the gun, stared directly into Fletcher's green eyes.

"I've seen what you can do. Back on the streets, in front of the hotel. You're like him," Fletcher jerked his head towards Beckett, "and people like him are power hungry, manipulative, and controlling. Tell me, why did you want the Digital Heart?"

"I'm not a garbagemancer, Fletcher. I... I just have working tech."

A low murmur carried through the room, whispers and exhaled breath. Cassidy looked around the room, more of Fletcher's revolutionaries had crowded in; surrounding them in a loose ring of bloody and sweaty bodies.

"You... you have what?"

"Ask Argyle. He has my EMF detector. It detects Electromagnetic fields, and was how I helped you find Beckett in the first place. I gave it to him to convince him to help me out." She paused to look at Argyle who was already nodding his head. "Isn't that right Argyle?"

The Rat took a shuffling step forward, his head bobbing an affirmative. "Yes, oh yes. Good tech," Argyle reached into his coat and pulled out the small, black box. Cassidy's heart sank.

Argyle held the EMF aloft, a crooked smile made out of his red slash of a mouth. The meter was broken, Cassidy could see it. The clear plastic covering was cracked, and the needle dangled, lifelessly within it. The faint sound of parts floating freely within the case floated to her ears.

"Show us," someone called from behind her and she cringed. *Dang*, Cassidy thought. *This isn't going to be good.*

Argyle made a quiet flourish with his hands and held the EMF in front of him, his face a mask of concentration that was soon marred by confusion and finally by frustration.

Slamming his open palm against the side of the device Argyle said, "It worked before. The little arrow would jump in place from left to right and back again." He gave it a furious shake, its loose innards rattling.

"So," the old medic said from her place kneeling next to Fletcher, "it worked when she gave it to you. Has it worked since?"

Argyle gave Cassidy a timid look, "Haven't used it."

"You can leave now, Rat." Fletcher's stare hardened once more, the gun in his hand steady and pointed directly at Cassidy. "Make sure he gets everything he was promised."

Argyle slipped out of the crowd; he gave Cassidy an apologetic look as he went. It wasn't obvious, but Cassidy thought she saw two burly men push their way through the crowd to follow him.

Once Argyle had left, Cassidy tried to make eye contact with Arturo, the kid. She gave him a wink, hoping to see even the barest smile hitch at the corners of his mouth, but he refused to look at her. He stayed close to Fletcher and watched the ground. Cassidy was alone.

"Not so hard to trick a simple-minded loner into thinking you have already working tech, I imagine," Fletcher's face twisted into a mocking grin. "And don't think I'm not grateful. You're right, you helped us out. More than any of us can really put into words." Fletcher looked around the room with an obvious nod of his head. The others there followed suit, all of them except Arturo and the medic.

"The issue isn't the what, but the why. So, let me ask you again: why did you help us?" More whispers cascaded through the crowd.

"It seemed like the right thing to do," Cassidy said, her shoulders slumped forward, her head down. "I just wanted to help you."

"And it had nothing to do with your own self-interests?"

"No."

"Not even for the Digital Heart?" Fletcher looked at her around the gun.

"Well… if I had known…"

"And why did you want the Heart so badly?"

"I… I can't…"

"Is it because you wanted to establish yourself as a garbagemancer?" Fletcher's voice was ramping up to a fever pitch. His voice was high and strained. Cassidy fought the urge to cover her ears.

"I'm not a garbagemancer," Cassidy felt her voice

quiver and hated the weakness in it; the acceptance of what was happening.

"Then why didn't you want to kill them?" Fletcher was in a rage, his voice echoed in the little room. Cassidy couldn't understand why the others didn't shield their ears and flinch away from Fletcher, from his anger.

"Listen to yourself," Cassidy said, her back straight and her fists clenched. "I didn't want to kill them because you don't just kill people for no reason! You don't kill people, especially when they are helpless." She could feel the heat on her face as her cheeks flushed red.

"That's very obtuse of you," Fletcher said. His voice had returned to its normal cadence so quickly that Cassidy had to look at him twice to make sure it was the same person. "Evil begets evil, Cassidy. If Beckett or his second in command live they'll attempt to take back their position – their power. Men like them, men who have become accustomed to power, can't live under someone else's rule. Worst of all, they have the abilities and influence to regain what they lost. They have allies." Again Fletcher looked around the room, his followers nodding in agreement. "No, these men and their allies need to be taught a lesson. They need to be taught that we are not afraid of them. That we will not be subject to their rule, to their whim."

A roar of approval rose over the crowd, and a satisfied smile curled Fletcher's lips. He kept his eyes on Cassidy for a moment, and she could feel the anger and the hate barely contained within. A thought rose in her mind, what happened to him?

Then he turned and fired two shots into Beckett and Harrison.

CHAPTER FOURTEEN

Cassidy managed to suppress the scream that bubbled up in her throat, but she couldn't control the flinch that came with each shot.

Guns were nothing new to her. In her line of work she had spent plenty of time navigating hostile governments that were covetous of their artifacts and their history. She'd dealt with drug cartels, terrorists, treasure hunters, and poachers. Cassidy had become good at negotiation, but that didn't mean it worked every time. She'd been fired at more than she cared to count, and she'd fired a gun – multiple guns. Cassidy didn't like being on either side of it.

The room echoed with the gunshots, and it drew those gathered closer. Cassidy shivered at their ghoulish interest in the wreckage Fletcher had just caused. She stood, transfixed on the aftermath but thankful the room crowded with onlookers that blocked her view. They pushed forward to get a better look, and to congratulate Fletcher.

A tug at the hem of her shirt woke Cassidy from her trance and she turned, thin fingers pried open her clenched hands. Her fist wrapped around something thin and sharp.

Argyle was stooped there, his brown eyes meeting hers briefly.

"Come," he said, his thin spider-like fingers grabbed Cassidy's wrist and pulled her out of the small kitchenette.

They moved through the old warehouse quickly, those revolutionaries that had remained outside the kitchenette now hurried passed them to see what had happened. None of them paid the odd pairing any heed.

"Fletcher has gone insane," Cassidy said when they had made it outside. Her hands were shaking, and she gnashed her teeth, what had she done? "How could I help him do this?"

Argyle sauntered around the back of Beckett's tractor trailer, a relic now like the rest of its brethren, his large eyes peering inside, scavenging. "It's not your fault," he said picking up a wayward nail he found in the truck bed and stuffing it in his oversized coat pocket. "He tricked you."

"Did he?" Cassidy turned on Argyle, her hands still in tight fists. "I was the one stupid enough to think his plans were selfless, to believe he wanted to better this world. You'd think I'd know better: all the things I've seen, all the places I've been."

"It happens," Argyle said and flicked away a cracked piece of plastic with a sneer. "When you make choices with your heart, it happens. Fletcher, he's a good talker. He knows how to say things that make him seem better. Beckett has some of that too. They pander to anyone willing to listen, twist them with their words. They make promises they can't keep and make sure their forked tongue is out of sight behind a smile. Argyle learned this; he learned this a long time ago. That's why he lives alone. Why he doesn't get involved. Why he helps only when he needs help."

"I can't do that. I can't live my life on the fence."

"With choices like this, what else do you have?" Argyle shrugged and bent his head to the floor of the truck bed, his eyes scouring it.

They both turned, noise erupted within the building. People were shouting, running.

"Maybe there's a third choice," Cassidy said and fumbled her hand within her satchel. "Argyle, can you take me to the old subway tunnels?"

"There are many ways to get to the subway," Argyle grunted.

"I need to get to the entrance close to a park. This section of park was one of Beckett's fake hideouts. Do you know it?" Cassidy said and clasped her hand on the Digital Heart.

Argyle nodded and turned his head sideways, his eyebrows raised.

Cassidy pulled out the artifact and studied it as it hung from her fingers. "Maybe there are other ways to end a war without favouring one side over the other."

A loud crash came from the building behind them, and more raised voices still too low to hear. But getting closer.

***

"Beckett used many underground hideouts," Argyle panted, his loping stride still surpassing Cassidy's own panicked run. "Only one was as you described it. A place long forgotten even before the Night the Lights Went Out."

The shouts of Fletcher's revolutionaries had died away, confined to Beckett's final hiding place as they fled. Cassidy thought she heard an agonized scream of rage as they pushed themselves out of sight of the squat warehouse.

"I hope you're right," she said, her legs aching as she pumped them to run through the formerly deserted streets of the strange New York.

They ran twenty blocks before Cassidy called a break and collapsed on the cracked asphalt and concrete. She leaned against a rough brick building and massaged her thighs, her fingers pushing hard into the muscles in hopes of waylaying the cramps she knew were coming. Argyle's shoulders heaved as he sucked in air, and though he leaned one hand on the same building, he remained on his feet. His eyes were vigilant of the space behind them.

"It's not much further, we need to hurry," he reached out a hand to help her up.

"Why are you helping me, Argyle?" Cassidy said and let herself be dragged upright. "I don't have any more tech to give you."

"No more tech needed," Argyle said and shook his long coat, the jangle of broken parts emanated from within. He smiled.

"Then, why?" Cassidy said as they started a slow walk. "It's bound to make your life more complicated."

Argyle shrugged, but his red slash of a mouth maintained its crooked grin.

They'd made it to the playground. The city was remarkably still and overpowered by an eerie silence. The broken-down pick-up truck kept a silent vigil over the abandoned lot, useless in its lack of menace. Cassidy let out a sigh of relief – finally something that she recognized. They were close.

In the vast cityscape from which Argyle had led her, Cassidy could hear the faint rise of voices. Distant, but they were getting closer.

"They can't know which way we went," Cassidy said looking over her shoulder. No sign of them yet.

Argyle grunted and pointed above her. Cassidy stared, the blue sky fading to a sickly orange. Something glinted in the distance, a patch of orange light that wavered like an eye that blinked to a strange rhythm.

"They had spotters?" Cassidy said and turned her focus back to running.

Argyle was silent save for his laboured breathing.

Of course they did, Cassidy thought, what else would Fletcher have the children do for his rebellion? Arturo was the only one she had seen at Beckett's, she had just assumed that the rest were at home, safe. That was before she'd seen Fletcher kill two men, before she knew how important the cause was to him, and what he would do to attain his goals. Having children use pocket mirrors to signal directions seemed like a negligible offence at this point.

They ran. Air fled their lungs, burning in a desire to rest. Argyle maintained a steady gallop, his stooped form unwavering. Cassidy pushed herself to keep up, but her body was on the verge of revolt. Her muscles screamed, pleading for rest and relief. As she pumped her legs, she could feel every muscle ripple and quiver, could feel them strain in protest. Cassidy was tired, overwhelmed, angry. And exhilarated. She welcomed the pounding of her heart, the fever pitch of her pulse. It was enough; she pushed herself onward.

It wasn't until something buzzed passed her in a blur of colour and left a stark gust of cool breeze in its wake that Cassidy realized they were riding bicycles. Another passed by her, its driver released a high-pitched ululation that might have been meant as a laugh. She looked over her shoulder and dozens of bikes were approaching, each driven by a revolutionary with a maniacal grin contained as if in rictus on their zealous faces. Baseball bats were held aloft as they zoomed towards Cassidy and Argyle. Where there weren't bats there were clubs made of everything from a table leg to a cane to a cracked off tree branch.

Cassidy lurched forward, thrown off balance by her quick turn, she fell forward as another bike passed her. It was a bike she recognized from her childhood - a BMX. Its simple handlebars on a slight angle forward, its seat set low so that the driver's knees came precariously close to their hands with each revolution of the pedals.

She rolled forward and got to her feet. They were all riding BMX bikes, customized to their liking, but there was no mistaking them. Cassidy could feel a giggle bubble up her throat, she was being chased by adults riding bicycles.

The air above her head was parted by a baseball bat

that sliced through as she was regaining her feet. Cassidy cursed, the remnants of the laugh left a bitter taste in her throat.

Up ahead, the two bicycles that had passed them were discarded, the drivers out of their seats and prepared to meet Argyle and Cassidy as they came. The bicycle that just swung at her was turning in a wide arc; coming around to make another pass.

"Kill the Rat," Fletcher's voice rose above the whizzing bicycle tires, "leave the girl for me."

Cassidy chanced another look over her shoulder, Fletcher was there, riding tandem with another on a customized banana seat with a long back bar. His beaten and bruised face was livid with excitement, Harrison's gun lifted above his head in exaltation.

"How many bullets do you have left in there?" Cassidy whispered as she ran toward the two waiting revolutionaries.

Argyle had gotten there before her, a snarl issuing from him as he leapt on the first of their welcome party. It was a big, broad man with one end of a chain wrapped around his forearm, swinging the other end lazily in large circles. His smirk turned to a grimace once the grim realization came over him that the Rat was not going to back down.

They rolled on the ground; the chain made useless at the close range. Still, the big man hadn't given up. He launched his lunchbox sized hands into Argyle's side and stomach. Argyle ignored the blows, his focus only on scratching and biting at the man, drawing blood wherever he could.

Distracted, Cassidy ran into the clutches of the other waiting revolutionary. He wasn't as large as the other man, but his thin limbs were strong and tight as if they were corded with carbon steel.

He grabbed her around the bicep and brought her around to face him, his strong fingers had dug deep into the soft inside of her arm and she winced in spite of herself. Her assailant smiled, and drew her into him. She was dangerously close to the man's shaggy brown beard when she heard a chuckle.

"Not so tough, eh girlie?"

He was taller than her, but not by much. He leaned closer, a snarl of a grin beneath his unkempt beard. With a grunt, Cassidy slammed her forehead into the man's nose. There was a loud crunch as she broke the cartilage and bone, and a spurt of blood shot from his nose; he released Cassidy. She knew that his nose was broken, that his eyes would start to water and blur, that blood would ooze, and he'd have a hard time breathing. He grabbed at his nose and freed Cassidy from his grip, cursing her.

Argyle ran past her, his face and hands streaked with blood, and she followed. The buzz of the circling bikes and the yelling assailants filled her ears as they ran. In the distance, she could see the tunnel entrance.

A red BMX passed her. The driver, a middle aged woman with swimming goggles over her eyes and a white streak that blew back with the rest of her long curly hair, was swinging a bat above her head. With a devilish smile, the woman howled and brought the bat down on Argyle's back, slapping across both of his shoulders with a sickening thud. Argyle stumbled forward, but kept his feet -- somehow.

Cassidy tried to push herself, tried to make her aching limbs go faster, to support Argyle and keep him on his feet. She tried to do that, but the bikes were faster.

Another bike passed, the medic who had tended to Fletcher's wounds at Beckett's hideout, a crowbar speckled with white paint held out to the side. The medic gave Cassidy a lazy wink as she sped forward and slammed the crowbar into Argyle's back. This time he fell.

Argyle landed on his hands and knees, his arms quivering against the strain to keep himself away from the ground. Cassidy knelt beside him, one arm thrown over his back and hands on his shoulders.

"Come on," she said and tried to guide him to his feet.

"No," Argyle growled, but he didn't shake off her hands as he stood.

The bikes began to circle.

"You go," Argyle said, his eyes following the bikes as they passed before him.

"That's stupid," Cassidy said, her eyes lingering on the tunnel entrance that couldn't have been more than thirty feet away. "We're so close."

Argyle nodded. "We'll never make it. You might," he said and pointed a finger at her.

"Don't be an idiot, we can both make it. Once we're in the tunnel they'll have to abandon their bikes. Single file. It will be easy."

"It's a good plan," Argyle stood straight, "you should use it."

The Rat sprang forward and grabbed a bike by its

frame, stopping it in its tracks. The driver, a small man with round glasses and a too thick moustache, was too surprised to act and fell off with a grunt when Argyle lifted the bike in the air.

"Go," Argyle yelled and threw the bike into the midst of those that still circled, knocking even more from their seats.

Cassidy didn't move. She watched Argyle as he repeated the same manoeuvre, dislodging more bikers as he did, but there were too many. For everyone he knocked over, there were two more waiting. They flanked him, and then swarmed. They forgot their bikes, but not their weapons, and went to work attacking Argyle.

When she finally unrooted herself, Cassidy made to follow Argyle into the fray, ignoring the time, the darkening sky, and the probability that Gamgee would block the portal and keep her in this reality forever.

"No," Argyle roared, his bulging eyes falling on her for a moment. He was holding his own, despite being outnumbered and unarmed. His lanky form slunk away from blows, but returned them with as much, if not more, gusto. Still, Cassidy knew it was only a matter of time. Argyle did too.

"Go," Argyle said again as he sidestepped an attack from a table leg. And he smiled. Not his nervous, twitching smile that he had given her when he first met her, or when he helped her escape just hours before, but a full, big, and pleased smile. A happy smile. "Go."

Cassidy ran.

CHAPTER FIFTEEN

The door swung open, its rusted hinges squealed in a unheeded protest, and Cassidy slipped into the dark tunnel beyond.

Argyle had kept them at bay, but Fletcher and his mob were on her heels and she was running out of time. In a moment of hesitation, Cassidy scoured the floor for something to jam up the door with, something to slide across the handle to delay its opening, but there was nothing but rat feces and dust. She cursed loudly. Not for the first time that day did she regret forgetting her shovel at Beckett's hideout.

The tunnel was gripped in shadows. A darkness that wouldn't have been fully pushed back even if the dead amber lights that spotted the curved ceiling had been working. Another curse was on her lips as she braved the darkness, her feet trying to follow the path she'd taken just a few days before; her memory would have to light the way.

It wasn't long before the echo of her running feet and hitched breath was joined by the metal scream of the door opening behind her. Cassidy could feel her heart hasten, her eyes grow wide, and her fists clench. She ran. She ran as fast as she could with the gibbering sound of an unruly gang flowing into the tunnel behind her.

The exit from the tunnel was open, a subtle glint of light helped Cassidy see the door frame as she leapt through it.

She was back in the subway tunnels, the tiled walls and iron tracks a welcome, familiar sight. Without slowing, she planted one hand on the precipice that stood guard over the tracks, pushed herself up and into a roll, before taking to her feet again. A grin slathered her face, "I can make it, I can make it," she said between harsh exhalations.

A crowbar smashed into the column she was running past, the subway tile exploded in a fine mist that caught one of Cassidy's eyes. She rubbed at it with her fist, large tears welling up to displace the irritant.

"We got her," a young man's voice crowed, from behind her an echo of breathless chuckles followed.

Cassidy waded through the subway, her balance offset while she dug at her eye. She had slowed, but it couldn't be helped. It was either that or fall onto the tracks or smash into a column. Judging by the growing roar, Fletcher's revolutionaries were close behind.

More objects were thrown at her, the former clubs now makeshift missiles launched with reckless abandon and bolstered by the original success of the crowbar. None since had been as successful and Cassidy hoped they littered the ground behind her, something to slow her pursuers down some.

She dodged past another column and flinched away

from a crossbow bolt that was dug into the tile. "Cross-bows. Great," Cassidy cursed and pushed on, pondering her worsening situation.

"Wait," she said aloud, "they didn't have crossbows." Cassidy tried to think back to the blur of events that brought her here. The image of Argyle's red slash of a mouth growing into a sincere and happy smile attempted to force its way to the forefront of her thoughts. Even so, she couldn't recall seeing any crossbows, or any bows for that matter.

Beckett's guards, she thought and chanced another smile. The grey coats who were acting as a decoy for their boss. The same guards that she ran afoul when she first slipped into this reality. The exact same shoot-first-ask-questions-later thugs that had managed to chase her away from the portal and into the arms of Fletcher and his cronies. The portal wasn't far now. She just had to hope she got there in enough time to vanish and not bring anyone with her.

The tracks sloped in a gradual curve and Cassidy started to recognize her path, even though she hadn't had much time to study anything on the way out. She caught sight of a particular piece of graffiti, a sprawl of letters as tall as she was. The neon colours were bright enough to make out even in the near dark of the subway tunnels. The Digital Heart. Cassidy clutched her satchel close to her and didn't see the figure appear from the shadows in front of her.

The man Cassidy bowled into had been equally un-aware of her and a loud yip escaped from him as they collided, his crossbow clattering to the floor.

"What the hell?" said another grey coat emerging behind the first, his crossbow firmly in his grip. Cassidy looked at each of them, they mimicked her. It was an unspoken stalemate, that Cassidy felt could have went on forever if the screams and howls of her pursuers didn't reach them.

"What the hell was that?" the first man said, picking up his crossbow.

"It was rebels, you idiots. Beckett sent me here to warn you they were coming. We're to hold them off until backup arrives," Cassidy said and pushed the two grey coats towards the sound of the oncoming gang. She saw more than confusion on their faces, but ran off before they had a chance to question her on it. Besides, they'd have their hands full.

Cassidy had no illusions that the two grey coats would stop Fletcher and his cronies for long, but it might give her just enough time to get through the portal.

She peeled through the hesitant darkness and was sure that the portal couldn't be much farther when she heard the curses of the two grey coats, and the unmistakable sound of crossbows launching. Screams followed, tinged with pain, anger, and fear. The crossbows that the grey coats carried looked top of the line. Hunter modifications, for the man that didn't want a challenge when he wanted to kill something. Cassidy knew the crossbows were easy for a quick reload. As long as the grey coats had some extra bolts on hand they'd do the job. But for how long?

That was the gamble. Cassidy pushed herself onward. Her legs were so tired that they squealed for rest and continued to threaten mutiny, but she gritted her teeth and bullied them on. She distracted herself by trying to count the number of bolts fired, the sharp twang of the crossbow string as it let a pointy stick fly.

Cassidy managed to count to ten before the rage fuelled roar of her pursuers took over. The grey coats let loose five each. Not bad. She tried not to think about what happened to them next.

Finally, after ten more minutes of running with everything she had left, Cassidy tumbled into the cavern where she'd originally entered this world. The less elaborate tags spouting the Digital Heart crawled to the ceiling. The darkness that settled there was almost complete, and she was reminded of Gamgee's mistaken assumption that it was some sort of cave.

"Wait 'til he hears about this," Cassidy said aloud, bent over to catch her breath, hands on her knees.

"Who?"

The voice rolled behind her, a languid and perfectly calm voice for someone who had followed Cassidy across the better part of New York. She turned to face Fletcher, her hands curled into fists, her legs (still trembling) prepared to run or leap, kick or knee; she turned to make an end of it.

"Who is going to hear about this?" Fletcher was by himself, aside from the gun he held down at his side. His misused face was swollen and bruised, scratches and cuts outlined a roadmap of the beating he had received at the hands of Harrison, the torture he'd been through, and still he was calm, confident.

"Where's the rest of your posse?" Cassidy backed up, a shimmer of hope that the portal would swallow her whole and she'd walk right into Gamgee, his head cocked in the study of some sort of anomaly or insect that had caught his eye. She wasn't that lucky.

"Oh, they're taking care of a couple of loose ends," he motioned behind him, a smirk on his face.

"You didn't want them to accompany you, didn't want them to see you get your ass kicked again?"

Fletcher laughed, a false bark that made Cassidy cringe. "Oh, it won't come to that will it, Cassidy?" He raised the gun.

"Let's say it doesn't," Cassidy tried on a smile that didn't seem convincing, "you don't want an audience to your triumph?"

Fletcher shrugged, "Why don't you just surrender. Give it up. We could help each other, with your powers and my vision, we would be unstoppable."

"I don't have powers, you idiot."

"Then how do you explain this?" Fletcher took her beaten, broken, and certainly dead phone from his pocket. "I can't quite figure how to turn it on, I suppose I'd need to have powers for that. Just like the piece of tech you gave that Rat we left back there…"

"I don't have powers, I just have working tech," Cassidy said, fighting the urge to punch Fletcher in his stupid beard, to hell with the gun in his hands.

"Really, and where do you get that?" Fletcher moved closer, the gun jabbed forward to emphasize each word. "Is the 'he' you spoke of earlier responsible for this tech?" Fletcher's calm facade dropped, replaced by a sudden and ferocious hunger. Spit flew from his mouth as he moved forward, a hesitance or barely held urge to jump forward.

"It doesn't matter, you'll never see it." Cassidy continued to back up, could feel her skin crawl and prickle in gooseflesh.

"Oh, I'm sure we can make you see reason," Fletcher cocked the hammer of the gun and took aim.

"Bye, Fletcher." Cassidy smiled and fell backwards.

The change in her surroundings was subtle, but it was there and it was familiar. It was the noise that did it, the distant sounds of traffic, conversation, movement. It was loud and bright and familiar. Also familiar was the pair of scruffy, ill-used brown loafers that she had landed next to. Gamgee gave her a wide-eyed look, a pocket watch in his hands, and his mouth agape.

"Cassidy, I had almost–"

"Blow it," Cassidy said, getting to her feet. "Shut the gate. Shut it now."

Gamgee spared her a sympathetic look (was there worry in there too?) before he twitched two fingers and nodded toward the darkness.

The explosion wasn't loud, just a small pop that was no louder than a cap gun Cassidy had used when she was just a little girl. The effect – well, it did the trick. The ceiling directly over the portal collapsed in a wave of debris and dust that left a mound of rocks blocking off the rest of the tunnel.

The portal was closed.

CHAPTER SIXTEEN

The first thing Cassidy did, once Dr. Gamgee and his hired specialists (a mechanical engineer, a retired demolitions expert, and the relaxed security guard they'd seen on their initial trek into the subway) had led her out of the tunnels, was buy a suite at the Hilton. Gamgee didn't argue, and offered up his credit card in the lobby.

"How was the trip?" Gamgee had said to her as they waited for the room to be made ready. "You were gone much longer than we'd anticipated," Gamgee said around a deep frown.

"I don't want to talk about it," Cassidy said and dug into her satchel. "Not yet."

She handed him the Digital Heart.

"A... a microchip," Gamgee held it in his palm, unsure of what to do with it.

"The Digital Heart," Cassidy said with a ghost of a smile on her face, and held up a hand to dissuade any further conversation. "We can talk about it later."

Gamgee nodded his ascent, but adjusted his glasses as he looked closer and closer at the microchip he had pinched between thumb and forefinger.

***

After a long, hot shower she lowered herself into the crisp, white linen of the king size bed and slept. She stayed that way for nearly twenty-four hours, her aching body had demanded it and she had gleefully succumbed.

Cassidy woke in the dark, a man stood in the shadows at the end of her bed with a gun in his hand. She thrashed about in her blankets, fighting the tangled sheets that grabbed at her arms and legs, and pushed herself to the floor to put the bed between her and the gun. Her breath came in harsh gulps, her heart beat in a rapid staccato, and she cursed between her teeth. Cassidy was unsure of how long she stayed on the floor, but her eyes were fully adjusted to the gloom before she poked her head over the side of the bed.

Nothing.

***

Cassidy stared out at the orange sunrise from the balcony of her room. Her elbows rested on the low metal table and she cradled a small mug of coffee between her hands. Since she had woken to the phantom of a dream (or was it a memory?) she'd set herself up out in the cool early morning air to take in the city. She took in a deep breath and expressed a slow sigh. The bright lights of the tall buildings and the noise of cars calmed her. The unnerving silence of the Dead World still clung to her, but it was fading.

EPILOGUE

Tallis turned and fired a shot behind him at those who were trying to get through the mining bay doors he'd sealed shut. There was one Xik'en pilot with him -- the one he'd taken the weapon from -- who was cowering a few feet to his side.

"Prepare it!" Tallis yelled, the Vao stones in the Branch of Languages on the left side of his face shimmered as it translated him, the golden nanotech wires cradling his jaw.

The inside of the mining bay was a maze of activity, with automated equipment going in every direction. Mechanical arms grabbed the massive hunks of asteroid when the mining pods dropped them after coming inside. Tallis stepped past its synchronized beauty without taking note of it, making a bee line for the craft he'd come for: the mining pod. When the pilot didn't follow he pointed the weapon at him and gestured him along. He did.

Emergency lights flashed as equipment overheated and got overloaded with material with no one to remove it.

Sirens blared in various tones, and Tallis had to fight

the urge to cover his ears as a result.

Forcing his captive to move, Tallis got himself under the hull of the mining pod and placed a steady hand on the open canopy. It opened at his correctly applied weight with a pressurized hiss. He smiled, motioned for the Xik'en pilot to join him, and then motioned to the controls: "Tell me how to fly it."

The Vao stones shimmered again.

***

Tallis' mining pod breached the environmental seal at a tight angle, revving immediately to top speed. Xik'en guards followed, breaking through the barrier he'd erected just as he left the station's atmosphere.

Within minutes the seasoned Xik'en pilots were in their stations and in hot pursuit, following the glowing blue trail of plasma Tallis' engines left behind. They were far behind but catching up, and there were only asteroids between him and the rest of space. They poured on the speed and followed him, knowing he had nowhere to run.

"Keep the fuel pod behind us," the Captain said, setting his visor's targets onto Tallis' craft. "If we follow until he's out of fuel, we will be, too. We'll need it to get back."

Tallis heard the command from within his own com link, the Branch of Languages translating it for him. He smirked and continued to push the gas as hard as he could, weaving between asteroids.

They stayed behind him for thirty-five miles, until the station was a small speck in the void behind them and they were clear of this side of the belt. There was nothing ahead but open space.

Tallis' wristwatch bleeped. He was lucky the Xik'ens hadn't taken it, that they had deemed it to be inferior mammal technology. He nodded as if it were speaking to him, and smirked. He turned his pod at a forty-five degree angle, veered downward, and prayed. "Got to hit it just right," he whispered to himself. "Just the right angle." He squeezed the stress ball between his left palm and the control stick.

"What's he doing?" the Captain said, lulled from the boredom of the steady course they'd been on and turning to follow. "There's nothing out here. Does he think we'll just stop?"

All at once, Tallis' ship blinked from existence before their eyes.

The Captain gasped. His ships sped toward the spot where Tallis had vanished, but none of them were at the exact angle, and they flew right by. The Captain turned around, breathless, unable to fathom what had happened.

ACKNOWLEDGEMENTS

The authors would like to pay special thanks to the *Slipstreamers* committee at Engen Books, including Amanda Labonté, Matthew LeDrew, AJ Ryan, Ellen Curtis, Erin Vance, and, Lauralana Dunne.

Without their tireless efforts, none of this would have been possible.

Special thanks to this episode's editor, Ali House.

Jon Dobbin would also like to thank his wife and children (Ashlee, Brianna, Thomas, and Conan), his parents, and Write Club. He would also like to thank Engen Books and their continued belief in him and his work.

COMING SOON!
NAVIGATING STORIES
BY JD RYOT & LISA M DALY!

The next incredible episode of Slipstreamers, Navigating Stories, will be available soon, written with the astonishing Lisa M Daly!

While searching for a strange magnetic mineral, Cassidy ventures to Vering Island, Astrada, a small island in a world at war with a tense relationship with the air base recently built on their island.

Relations between the islanders and the air base are already tense, but when Cassidy crash-lands it results in the air base taking something of great importance from the islanders to help the war effort.

Can Cassidy set things right on this world plagued by war before it's too late?

ON SALE NOW FROM ENGEN BOOKS

"Dunne breathes life into a world of magic and lore that will draw the reader in right up to the epic conclusion. Ashes is a heroic tale not to be missed."
Amanda Labonté
bestselling author of Supenatural Causes

When fifteen-year-old Phoenix loses her caregiver, everyone that she has ever known inexplicably turn their backs on her. Given the impossible burden of repaying an unknown debt, Phoenix sets out on her own with her trusty donkey, Muler, as her only companion.A chance encounter with Malcourt, a mysterious traveller, not only saves her life, but sets it on a trajectory that she would have never thought possible.

Jon Dobbin is an award winning author living in the St. John's, Newfoundland metro region.

He is a father of three, the husband to an amazing wife, an educator, and a tattoo and beard enthusiast.

Dobbin's work has appeared in the *Terror Nova, Chillers from the Rock, Dystopia from the Rock, Pulp Science-Fiction from the Rock, From the Rock Stars,* and, *Kit Sora: The Artobiography* collections. In 2019 he released his first novel, *The Starving.* In 2020 he released his second novel, *The Broken Spire.*

Quest for the Digital Heart is his first novella aimed at a Young Adult audience.

JD Ryot is the reclusive creator of the *Slipstreamers* series from Engen Books. JD is an avid fan of young adult literature and adventure serials. When asked if they had come to this world through a portal themselves, JD Ryot refused to answer. No record of their birth has ever been found... on this world.